LITTLE VISIBLE
DELIGHT

LITTLE VISIBLE DELIGHT

Edited by

S.P. Miskowski
Kate Jonez

Omnium Gatherum
Los Angeles CA

Little Visible Delight
Edited by S.P. Miskowski
and Kate Jonez

Anthology Copyright © 2013
Individual stories copyright by individual authors

ISBN-13: 978-0615932248
ISBN-10: 061593224X

First Edition

Table of Contents

"My love for Heathcliff resembles the eternal rocks beneath: a source of little visible delight, but necessary. Nelly, I am Heathcliff— he's always, always in my mind..."

—Emily Brontë, *Wuthering Heights*

INTRODUCTION

When Kate Jonez asked if I would be interested in co-editing an anthology of dark fiction I said yes at once. As soon as we began to talk about a theme we found we were in agreement. We wanted a collection of stories by writers whose work has dazzled us recently. And we wanted a common theme that would not limit the scope of the individual authors.

If you search 'obsessions and compulsions' online you'll find the list of references begins with diagnosis and therapeutic information. Check the same topic on any book site and nearly all of the titles will belong to self-help manuals. For most people, obsession is a scary subject, a disorder, a condition to be checked and controlled. It implies danger, poor judgment, diminished perspective, even madness.

Yet where would writers be without the depth of awareness that comes from studying one object, image, emotion, or idea intimately and relentlessly? In a sense, a writer's job is to be obsessed, to imagine something so intensely that its substance, its existence, is accepted and not questioned by readers.

Kate and I decided to let the contributors explore their own obsessions, whether personal, literary, or both. The central theme of *Little Visible Delight* is the irresistible, undeniably dark, potentially maddening, yet essential concept to which an author returns time and again. These are the stories conjured in the minds of writers when you ask them, 'What are you *really* thinking?'

Welcome to our obsessions.

The Receiver of Tales

Lynda E. Rucker

A letter arrives in the mail. That in itself is unusual enough. She had not realized people wrote letters any longer. She had not imagined anyone wrote anything any longer; isn't everything now encrypted in bits and bytes, nebulous as the spoken word? Schrödinger's writing; does it even exist if it isn't printed? She has never owned a personal computer, won't touch the things outside of work where she has to, can't abide them. First the future and now the present are passing her by. She is a thing of the past, and she knows it.

The envelope, dull and plain and white, tapped through the mail slot of the front door of the house she lives in, bears no identifying marks; its stamp is uncanceled.

She waits until she is back in her apartment to open the letter with trepidation and unfold the single sheet inside, upon which is scrawled in an unknown hand a single word: 'Soon.'

The world reels about her.

~

She is sick of all the stories she has to tell.

Not all of them are tragic, although the tales people feel compelled to share during the dark nights of their souls tend to have elements that are not the most uplifting. It isn't the substance of the stories, though, but the act of hearing them and writing them down that has grown tiresome. She feels like the ancient mariner, clawing at wedding guests and rambling on about an albatross, only she is begging others for their stories, not telling them herself.

Afterward, she writes them down and now her fingers are permanently ink-stained. Ruben's fingers had looked like that as well, she recalls; only paint— instead of ink-stained. She has to tell herself he'd not known what he was doing when he pushed the painting under the door of her little studio apartment in the old Victorian, where only a thin wall divided her place from his. The painting had made a scraping noise across her floor, and she'd jumped up, opened the door and looked down the long hallway and seen no one.

"Who's the girl that listens to the Pixies all the time?" said the attached note. It hurt to remember Ruben, and she hadn't listened to the Pixies in twenty-five years.

"I'm Aisha. The Pixies girl," she said to him the next day, her knuckles dropping away from the door because he answered it before she could knock. In her other hand she held the painting, swirls of doomsday oranges and red, a dying sun obliterating a blistering landscape. Ruben waved it away.

"It was a gift," he said. "Keep it." His eyes were red and moist. She thought he looked like someone who had not slept for a very long time.

Is this the story I'm writing now? Aisha asks herself. If so, this is a wonder indeed. What happens when the storyteller tells her own story? Doesn't it stand to reason that this will be the last one? What a blessing that would be, if she still believed in blessings. And the story surges out of her.

~

This was Ruben: a shock of dark hair (she'd always thought he looked like Nick Cave), an incessant parade of identical black T-shirts, the smell of cigarettes (unfiltered Lucky Strikes), a voice that sounded too deep to belong to the weedy boy in possession of it, and paint spatters, everywhere, on his forearms, his rumpled jeans, even on the rough hardwood floor of his apartment. "You'll have to pay for that when you move out," she said, and he just shrugged.

The old house off Boulevard had been chopped into six tiny apartments decades earlier: all day and all night long you heard your neighbors walking, arguing, fucking, sobbing, cooking, watching television. It was a shocking kind of intimacy, if you thought about it: Aisha, who had grown up with two sisters and two brothers, had nonetheless never experienced less privacy. Ruben dug it. He would lie for hours, he said, one ear to the floor, absorbing the lives that echoed beneath him. At first she didn't believe him, who would, but later that would be the least of the difficult things to believe. But she had to believe all of it. By then she'd seen— no, heard— too much.

~

"Aisha," he said. "What kind of name is that? I've never heard it before."

"I don't know. It was the name of my mom's best friend, but she died when my mom was pregnant with me. So I was named after her." Even before birth, someone else's past had claimed her.

"Oh." Ruben regarded her with those steady grey eyes. "That's wild."

He said it so softly, and she couldn't figure out what he meant by it. What would be wild about it? Later she would wonder whether his ever-abstract way of speaking was something he possessed before or if the vagueness had come upon him over time as it had with her. Sometimes she saw herself as others must see her, a frizzy-haired woman of indeterminate age, arms and legs covered on even the hottest day, speaking in a voice so soft it barely rose above a whisper with words that escaped her so often she would sometimes stand silent for minutes at a time. Nothing, she had learned over what seemed like an endless lifetime, made people quite so uncomfortable as a stretch of silence, particularly when you stood in front of them and presented them with that silence.

Uncomfortable at first, at least. Before long, they would be telling her their darkest, most painful secrets, the things they tried most to keep hidden away from the people who loved them, the stories that poisoned their lives if they allowed themselves to think of them at all.

She still lives in the chopped-up house on Boulevard. Over more than twenty years she has scratched and scrawled words on every surface from floor to ceiling. She dwells in a palace of ink. Words upon words and stories upon stories. She will not do as Ruben did; she will not weaken; she will not take the easy way out; she will not infect others as he infected her.

Ruben had tried to paint the virus out of himself but it got him in the end. She will never forget the sight of his body swinging in the incongruous sunlight that spilled through the window of his apartment. She stood aghast in his doorway for what seemed like hours. She did not scream or cry. She took in the swirling dust motes, the bluebottle fly dashing itself against the window, the heat of the room and the smell that had brought her to use the key he'd entrusted her with. It was summer. A perfect summer's day. In her nightmares it is always summer.

~

She burns the envelope and the paper that came with it in the enameled bathroom sink. The flames, flaring briefly, scorch the word that appeared there. Later she stands naked and shivering under the jets of hot water from the shower. She had to give up lovers long ago, when she began carving the stories into her flesh. Beautiful expanses of scar tissue cover her arms and legs, her stomach, her breasts, the tops of her feet.

She isn't Ruben. She won't weaken like he did. Ruben had been too afraid of the stories in the end. He'd tried getting away from the words, painting them out of himself instead— wasn't a picture worth a thousand words, after all— but they were stronger than he was. She, on the other hand, has entered into what she thinks of as an uneasy détente with the stories. She takes them into every part of her, literally into her very flesh, and in turn she is left alone. Or she always had been. Until now.

She remembers how timid Ruben had been. She'd worried about him, cooped up in his apartment all day. How did he get by? What did he live on? She'd never asked; he'd never told, and his death revealed no answers. No family came by, and the landlord, who hadn't known they were close, failed to mention he was hiring a cleaning crew to haul Ruben's effects to a dump. Coming home from class, she'd encountered them on a final haul and was able to save no more than a handful of his sketches.

She'd toyed briefly with the idea of moving into his apartment after he died, partly because she felt surprisingly bereft without him and partly because she felt sorry for the landlord who couldn't rent the place. But it was a college town, memories are short and cheap accommodations hard to come by. Soon enough a steady parade of kids rotated through the studio next door that she's never stopped thinking of as Ruben's.

Nobody stays there long, but that might be coincidence. College students move around a lot, after all.

His ghost isn't there; she knows that much for sure. She'd have been the first to know. After all, no one's stories were as compelling as those of the dead, and no needs so compelling as theirs to tell all before moving on. The dead Ruben seemed to have no stories; she supposes she would have none, either. Eating the tales of others leaves you with none of your own.

Haunted, the house is for certain, but every place is haunted, as is every person, and you need only to look into their eyes to see how much. Everyone grows more haunted with age but not every old person is more haunted than every young person.

She'd been lucky in her job, clerical work in the basement of a building on campus where she rarely comes into contact with other people and is left alone as long as she keeps her head down and gets things done. So they think she's a weirdo. The student workers in particular she imagines regarding her with horror. The brighter they burn the more she frightens them. *She is what I will turn into if I make the wrong choice. If I take the wrong classes. If I take the wrong job. If I take the wrong relationship. If I don't do the right things.* Most of them were too young to understand that all the right things in the world might not save them in the end.

At work, all day, she catalogues, she files, she makes photocopies and fills out forms and hits 'send' on emails. Things tick along regularly and predictably and twenty-odd years ago she'd never have imagined that such regularity, such boredom, such routine, could move her to tears of relief. The safety and security of it all. The way it buffers her against the world outside.

The world outside, and the thing that is drawing nearer to her. Sometimes she dreams of its footfalls in the corridor outside her apartment. Sometimes it taps on the window to be let in. Alone in her fortress of words she recites poetry to keep it out. The intoxication of the language seizes her, and she finds herself speaking in tongues, the verse of the ancients, the verse of forgotten people and lost races, the stories that had been lost.

Something is coming to retrieve them, and she does not want to let them go.

~

Everyone had thought she and Ruben were lovers, but they were not. The thought had never crossed their minds, in fact; they were something better. They were best friends. Despite the little they'd known about the mundane details of one another's lives like where they came from and what they'd been like before and who their parents and families were, they couldn't have been closer. They went in drag to parties, dressed in one another's clothes, answering only to the other's name. One bright morning they'd woken in the cemetery across from campus with no memory at all of how they'd gotten there the night before. Shaking with laughter at having eluded the sexton, they stole flowers from the graves to wear in their hair and ran all the way down to the Bluebird Café for a breakfast of omelets and big dense biscuits with apple butter. Later, after he died and the gift passed to her, she'd wondered at first how he'd managed to sleep in a cemetery at all with the dead all about, but she'd quickly learned that of course there are no ghosts in cemeteries; why would they linger in a place that had no meaning to them?

She hadn't understood then why Ruben gobbled hallucinogens like they were aspirin, acid and mushrooms and ecstasy, building a tolerance so high he started joking he had to keep them in his system just to stay in touch with reality. It wasn't a joke. What had been such a carefree time for her had been a final, desperate, losing bid for survival on his part. In the end, she hadn't been enough to save him.

~

Another letter comes through the mail slot, exactly one week later. This time she is standing in the lobby when it is pushed through, having just arrived home from work. She freezes as the flap clinks; she did not see anyone behind her as she came up the walkway, and she immediately tugs the door open, but the walkway is empty, and so is the sidewalk beyond.

She carries the letter up to her studio and sets it on the little table in the kitchen while she boils pasta and dumps some jarred sauce into a pan to heat. Then she sits and looks at the letter for a long time.

The last time she had received letters like these, Ruben had just died. At first she hadn't understood what was happening to her. His curse had come to her first in dreams, dreams that belonged not to her but to other people. There is, she learned, no mistaking other people's dreams for your own. It's not the content but the substance that is wrong, the grammar of other people's subconscious. It was a horrific violation, and she woke sick and unable to get out of bed. She'd failed all her classes that semester and never made it back into school, but by then it didn't matter anyway; where would she have gone, what kind of life could she have built with this inside her?

The first message had arrived shortly after, dropped through the slot just like the last by someone who was clearly not the mail carrier, who came into the building properly with a key and left the mail for everyone stacked on a shelf in the foyer. The handwriting was shaky and old-fashioned. Five mundane words: *He gave you his gift.* She dropped it, shuddering. Out loud she said, "You might as well say 'he gave you smallpox,'" but she didn't laugh after she said it like she'd hoped she might. She tried to be normal. She put on music and dressed up and went out to hear music like she and Ruben would have done together, but rather than trying her luck among the slim pretty girls and the earnest scruffy-haired boys she found herself slouched against the bar while a sad woman named Melanie rattled off a lifetime litany of abuse and bad luck to her. Melanie was pretty, dark-haired and dark-eyed, but this was not the kind of intimacy she was looking for; this was raw and shocking and real. Still, she misunderstood it, and took Melanie home with her, and woke in the night to find her crouched at the foot of her bed staring at her. "There's something inside you," Melanie said. "Something's wrong." She dressed and left and Aisha never saw her again.

She had begun to simultaneously attract and repel people like that; she knew it. They wanted her for the space of their stories and then no more. She somehow had not noticed she'd been Ruben's only friend, because they'd been so close there'd been space only for the two of them in the intense few months they spent together. That's how Ruben had known. How he had known he could let go and give it to her. She told herself it was not a betrayal. She told herself Ruben had not done it to hurt her. She told herself Ruben had done it because he'd known she was stronger than he could ever be.

But these days, she feels twice her age even if she looks half it. She feels the stories now are writing themselves upon her organs, that if she were sliced open, her heart and her liver and her bones would be covered in words.

~

In those early days, there had been two more letters in quick succession and then none until it all started up again. The second had been another single word framed by the expanse of creamy white all around it: 'Atavistic.' Well, that was helpful. She was a throwback. A shaman. She could hang herself a shingle and charge money and promise to channel people's spirit guides and go on television and weep while holding the hands of the mothers of lost children. The third was an actual letter, two pages covered in the shaky old-fashioned handwriting. She'd read it through once and burned it, willing herself to forget most of it. Over the years she had regretted her actions many times, but what was life made of if not hasty actions and years of regret? If she'd learned nothing else from all the stories she'd heard, she'd learned that.

The third letter had been an apology, of sorts. Or so she thought. Its language had been so elliptical. It had been like reading the writing of someone who not only lacks English as a first language but lacks facility with any language at all. She had burned it because it did not shed any light on her circumstances, on the hows and the whys. And yet there might have been clues in the letter, clues that in those early days passed her by.

~

She cannot bring herself to open the most recent letter, not after more than two decades of silence from them, whoever they are. That night in her apartment, the pasta had boiled over and the sauce had burned to the bottom of the pan while she sat and stared at it. She went out and bought a pack of cigarettes and smoked half of them, still staring at it, telling herself with each one she would open it *now now now*. She went out a second time and bought a bottle of wine and drank it down but she'd known better; as with Ruben, such substances barely touched her. In fact, afterward she felt more alert and on edge than before.

She carries the letter to work with her the following day; afterward, she sits in the sun outside a restaurant on Broad Street, which is choked with traffic. She needs to be in the world in order to confront what is inside the envelope.

She raises her head and looks all about her. *The trouble is, the town has changed and I have not. Everything has changed except me.* All the old stories are right; eternal life is a curse, not a blessing. Only the words carved on her flesh mark the physical passage of time. However ancient she feels in her soul, when she looks in the mirror she sees only a slightly maddened version of the Aisha that she's always been. The past twenty-five years have been agony; how many more quarter-centuries can she bear to count off before she gives up? How many had Ruben endured? How had she, who believed herself his truest intimate, known so little of the truth about him?

For now, her family jokes about her hiding a picture in the attic to ensure eternal youthfulness, or sleeping in a bed of graveyard dirt, but how long will it be before she will have to cut ties entirely and move on, disappear? And how *does* one disappear any longer? It's not like in ages past: a name change, a new town, a new country even, and a whole new identity. The modern world ensures your identity clings to you as surely as your fingerprints.

And then there is the hunger; oh, God, the hunger for people's stories, and how it mingles with repulsion until she is unable to distinguish one from the other. The insatiable lust for the most troubled or repellent pieces of people's past leaves her shaken and ashamed and starving for more. She knows what she is: it might not be blood that she drinks, but the effects are the same save for the fact that she does not leave a trail of dead behind her. No, if anything, she is the victim, not them.

Enough.

In one swift move, she rips the letter open.

~

My Dear Aisha,

She recoils at the first three words. How dare they call her by name. How dare they refer to her as 'dear' anything, as 'my' anything. Whoever they are, she is not theirs.

A quarter of a century has passed since our brother, whom you knew as Ruben, chose to finish his association with our order and left us a sister in his place.

No. No. No. She is a sister to four siblings she loves; she is not sister to these monsters, whoever they might be.

We find that a quarter of a century tends to be something of a turning point, the stage at which our new acolytes begin to seek answers about the why and the what next of who they are.

A vampire identity crisis. But of course. The ultimate ailment for the modern age.

The first and most important thing that we want you to know is that you are far from alone. And that you have a choice.

Those words are the most surprising words she's encountered so far. She rereads them a few times to make sure that she understands them.

You have a choice.

She reads on.

~

Alone that evening in her apartment, she thinks about the letter, and the choice. Ruben had presumably been offered this same choice at some point; why then had he not taken it?

Giving back the words...

She can relinquish it all. She can let go of the words; abandon the eternal life; return to a normal existence. No more stories, no more solitude, no more hunger. A life, a family, everything she has wanted across these years, all of those things that had been denied her for so long.

In the shower, she huddles under the hot water spray and weeps, clutching her scars, willing them away, the words carved there. By tomorrow, they will be gone. The walls of her apartment will be pristine again. Her mind, her insides, her soul will be cleansed. It will be as though it never was.

For the first time in twenty-five years, her dreams that night are undisturbed.

~

Yet she wakes in a panic, not knowing why. The first thing she does, even before opening her eyes, is clutch at her flesh, pinching it and running her fingers over it, but it is too late. Her body is smooth and unblemished. The scars that have marked her for well over a decade are gone.

She is still dreaming. She must still be dreaming. She keeps her eyes clenched tight, willing the dream to end, but it does not. It will end on waking. She must open her eyes. It must be near midday, because the room is flooded with light, and her walls are cream-colored, her words gone.

"No," she says. "It isn't right. It isn't fair. It isn't what I wanted."

She says it hoping they can hear her— whoever they are— after all, had they not heard her desires, what she believed to be her desires, of the previous night?

But she was wrong. Whoever they were, why could they not have seen that, the desire behind her desire, the gap between what she believed she wanted and what she truly wants?

She dresses quickly, and clatters down the stairs. She was due at work hours ago, but work doesn't matter any longer. Outside, she staggers toward Prince Avenue. There has to be someone out here who needs to share a story. But passersby ignore her, or seem to actively avoid her, and no wonder: she must seem crazy to them. It is all she can do not to clutch at them, shout at them to tell her their stories, to pour their pain into her and let its sweetness consume her.

Then she does grab a man by the shoulders— he has a story, a terrible one, she can tell from the eyes, she still has that much of her old self, at least— but he only stares at her, shakes her off with a 'Crazy bitch!' and goes off muttering about her, glancing back once or twice to ensure she keeps her distance.

That's when she starts to weep, and to push up the sleeves on her shirt to stare again in horror at her unbroken flesh. Had this, then, been the moment that had destroyed Ruben? Not the burden, but its loss?

But *where* have her stories gone? Who has taken them on? Who has her power now? Why was she not allowed to choose a successor as Ruben had been? Was it because she loved no one as she and Ruben had loved each other?

No one answers, because they aren't speaking to her any longer. She is no longer of any concern to them.

~

The woman at the rental car counter is tanned and perky. Aisha watches as she efficiently taps out codes on the computer keyboard. No insurance, thanks, back in a week (never), and she runs Aisha's debit card and hands over the keys and just like that Aisha is free, freer than she's ever been in her life. She points the car west and drives. Near dusk, she stops at a Denny's and eats a grilled cheese sandwich with fries, then gets back in the car and drives until she can't any longer. She isn't sure where she is when she pulls over to sleep for a while. In the morning she decides to get her bearings and purchase a paper map at the next service station.

Surely ghosts will still speak with her, even if the living will not. Surely she can find sites of savagery and mass suffering, Indian massacres and Civil War battlefields. Surely the dead will want her.

She has made a series of turns so far off the beaten path that she drives for some time without seeing any services or even a main road at all, and the gas gauge is dropping. Twice she stops at isolated houses and knocks on the door in hope of asking for directions but no one answers; at one, she hears a television inside, but perhaps she wouldn't answer a door to a stranger either, if she lived in the middle of nowhere.

(And yet she would, or she would have; letting in strangers was what she *did*. What she did now, who she was now, she could not say.)

At last a series of turns brings her onto a wider road, and then a three-lane highway. A gas station comes into view just as her gauge is slipping into the red zone. She fills up the car, and although there aren't any maps for sale, she gets directions back onto the interstate from the owner. She is, it seems, somewhere in Arkansas.

Hunger, not for food, gnaws at her like the pain of a phantom limb.

Ruben's fate is not going to be her own. She doesn't need them, whoever they are. She can still get people to tell her their stories and she will learn how to hear ghosts on her own as well. She will figure out how to survive. Money, a place to live, those things are easy enough to come by. She just needs to get people's words. She just needs to disappear. For all she knows she might live forever after all.

Before she reaches the interstate again, she sees a small figure trudging along the side of the road, and she eases the car onto the shoulder. What she'd taken for a teenage boy is actually a girl of roughly the same age, a pale face ringed by jet-black hair peering out from a hoodie.

"I'll make you a deal," she says as the girl approaches her driver's window, mouth opening to query or beg. Aisha nods at the keys still in the ignition as she slides over into the passenger's side. "You drive. Anywhere you want to go. I'll sit here and you tell me about yourself. Tell me your story."

The girl hesitates. Aisha sees her looking for the catch; glancing around half in expectation of an assailant, furtively surveying the back seat, assessing the situation.

"No strings attached," says Aisha, "take it or leave it," inside, begging the girl to take it.

The girl presumably makes the split second decision that this is one gift horse she will not look in the mouth, shrugs a little at whatever fates she's consulted, and opens the driver's side door. "You can drive, can't you?" Aisha says, and the girl nods and, surprisingly safety conscious, goes through the motions of adjusting the seat, the seatbelt, the rear and side mirrors before cautiously easing them back onto the road.

"Anywhere?" she says, and her voice is a backwoods drawl.

"Anywhere at all," Aisha says. "I've got all the time in

the world. But remember your end of the deal. Before we get to where you want to go, you have to tell me your story."

Aisha lies back against the headrest and closes her eyes. The girl begins to talk, and above the comforting throb of the engine her accent and her story are as dark and as murky as the swampland she describes as her eastern Arkansas home. But there is some measure of hope in the story she tells as well; hope drove her out of the house one moonless night, after all; hope had her stick out her thumb in search of rides, hope made her get into Aisha's car and start driving toward a destination not yet named, but that didn't matter, because her story in all its pain and glory is spilling out of her and Aisha is right: she doesn't need *them*. The girl talks and talks and Aisha devours the words; she finds a ballpoint pen in the glove compartment of the car and begins writing them in tiny letters on the palm of her hand and when she runs out of room she moves to her forearm and when there is no more room there she moves to her knees, her calves, and the girl doesn't seem to care because they never do once their stories get going. In the midst of the terror and despair of which they speak, the stories are beautiful. The words make them beautiful. The fact that a living tongue spoke them makes them beautiful. Aisha cannot wait to live inside them again, to ruin her flesh with their substance again, and what will become of her now she does not know, but she also knows that it does not matter because the stories will always be, written on her bones, the very filaments that string her soul together and keep her anchored to this earth.

Author's Note: Lynda E. Rucker

This story appears to be about compulsions that affect all of us who write— an obsession with storytelling— but that wasn't where it began or the compulsion I meant it to be about. The actual compulsion that sparked the story for me is setting and sense of place, and my ruthless mining of my own past to fold those memories into fiction.

I connect very strongly with places; places I have loved simultaneously anchor me in a very physical sense and obsess me in a powerful, transcendent way. The settings in much of my fiction are deeply personal to me. Furthermore, I have always had very little sense of the past as past; time seems to me without linearity and places and events from years ago can seem realer to me than something from last week or last month, and so places that I have left remain very present to me.

So this started out as a story about a place I love, and have left behind twice— Athens, Georgia— and the uneasy relationships people have with the past and how those pasts consume their present. That it ended up being all about storytelling as well is, I suppose, inevitable, because the past, after all, is in the end nothing more than the stories that we tell ourselves.

Needs Must When the Devil Drives

Cory J. Herndon

I

The man I meant to kill wouldn't be home for another thirteen and a half minutes. The original plan called for a full thirty just to be safe, but the actual preparation wouldn't take more than five. I like to show up early. Even so, I was running late, but still had time to set an ambush.

I hadn't seen his grubby apartment building in years. It hadn't changed a bit. I was counting on that, in fact, because I'd given up my front door key when I moved out. Hadn't given it a second thought at the time; who knew I would be back here after so long needing to kill a man? But even the slight risk Art the building manager might notice me was too much risk, so going through the front door was out anyway. He might recognize me.

Art the building manager was why I was running late. He made me waste almost ten minutes hiding around the corner while he yammered away at one of the building's hapless tenants, but finally he released the poor young woman from his conversational grip and strolled out the door, down to the corner, and into his favorite tavern. The grubby handyman would be there for the rest of the day and most of the night. He'd probably end up passed out in his ground floor office by three a.m. and might even make it to the ratty old cigarette-burned couch he kept there.

No, I did not need questions from Art. He would maneuver in front of the only exit, light up a pocket-flattened, generic cigarette, and launch into his specialty— aimless and endless small talk. Ask about the weather, ask about the game, pontificate on politics he didn't understand and never would. Back when I lived here, I smoked like a chimney. When I smoked, I smoked outside because who wants that shit all over everything you own? Not me. I didn't have much, but I didn't need it coated with tar like my lungs. Art would bum a few cheap Basics from me now and then, after the building owner made him stop lighting up in the office.

I never talked to Art about any of my real interests, any of my real studies. But we did converse, at sometimes interminable length, about nothing of real interest. Sports, weather, the ass on that girl, the news at eleven, maybe one more cigarette. I damn near decided to stop off later and kill him too, just for good measure, but killing Art would be fatally stupid. Art wasn't the guy who had to die.

No, the clock being punched today resided in apartment 304. Didn't matter how I did it— it just had to be done or I was royally fucked. Up the fire escape I went.

The ladder was a bit rusty, but the ludicrously narrow space between my old building and the bathhouse next door concealed the blatant breaking and entering I was about to commit, as well as what must have been a pretty undignified ascent when viewed from below. The worst part of the interminable two-story climb was my increasingly labored breathing. I was no longer a young man. After so many years of planning, I could still blow this thing for want of lung-power.

At sixty-seven I got pretty asthmatic with anything more strenuous than a brisk walk, but rather than admit it and get help for it, help I could easily afford, I just got better at avoiding anything close to exercise. I quit a two-pack-a-day smoking habit a few years ago when fear of death finally overcame physical need. I figure I'd earned a little more time, time I used to find the precise man I had to kill.

But it didn't make it any easier to ascend two stories on a fire escape.

By the time I got to the window— unlocked, since Art had *never* gotten around to putting locks on the windows— I damn near passed out. Some part of my brain cursed me for not bringing an oxygen tank like I was hiking goddamn Mount Everest, another part reminded me to breathe in through the nose, out through the mouth. Best way I knew to get the breathing under control without an inhaler.

I checked my watch. Only four minutes left. Time to move.

I knew the window had no working lock, so there was nothing to prevent me from pressing my palms against the glass, gently pushing up, and sliding the window open except the handiwork of Art the building manager. Over the years he'd unprofessionally slathered so much paint onto the windowsill and the window frame that the two had, in fact, joined together via the rubbery medium of lead-filled paint that never quite seemed to dry. No one had ever cut the paint with a razor to allow the window to open, either. This bastard had been living in a sealed apartment for months because he couldn't be bothered to hit the shaving aisle at the Shop Rite.

When the paint finally gave way the cracking and popping was loud enough to make me freeze, but the rest of the city went on with its business. Car horns blared; a school band practiced up the street in the hot spring day, a homeless guy charmed the pocket change from a pair of young passersby. The hiss of the bus arriving at the stop half a block away drowned them out, the same bus I'd ridden to my undergrad classes when I was younger. An episode of *Oprah,* a game of *Super Mario World,* and Blondie's 'Call Me' all fought for clarity through open windows above my intended victim's floor. No sounds of sudden alarm, no downward-gazing faces popping out to scream when they saw what I was doing.

The window slid open easily once the seal broke. The apartment smelled like the bachelor's home it was, infrequently occupied and carelessly rotten. Dishes stacked for longer than was hygienic, stale cigarettes, the posters and writing and tobacco stains on the walls— okay, it took me back. If it wouldn't have given me away two minutes and thirty seconds before the big event, one of the Camels in the pack on my intended victim's desk would've been half-smoked by now.

Even with the window wide open, I found it tricky to slide feet-first into the living room from the inconveniently placed fire escape. The musty carpet inside muffled my awkward landing. Two minutes. The original plan was out of the question now. No time to find the right chemicals, to make it happen quickly, to spare my victim much pain. He was going to suffer, and there was no way to avoid it now. Needs must when the devil drives.

Needs must when the devil drives. I heard someone say that on a TV show once in this very building. Useful phrase. Sounded more noble— if less accurate— than 'the ends justify the means.'

I had no clue what would happen now, but I knew what *had* to happen if I was going to get out of that apartment alive. The man had to die. He would have to die as quietly as possible, and quickly, too. Painless wasn't going to happen.

Needs must when the devil drives.

One minute, thirty seconds. Time to be quiet. Time to be quick. Time to find a weapon. Maybe relying on this place to have a ready murder tool close at hand was asking too much. The closet? No. The kitchen. Where the knives were.

Quick and quiet. This guy had to own at least one damned knife. It would be messy, but it might work. It *would* work. There they were, on the grimy counter, a block of cheap wood impaled by an incomplete set of cheap-ass

Ginsu-style knives. Not even the Ginsu brand but knock-offs. Two or three of them were missing and all the steak knives were gone— too bad, something that size would've been easier to use. The carving knife and a bread knife were still there. The carving knife was thin, almost flimsy, but when clutched a certain way— elbow bent, blade horizontal— it was pure Norman Bates. Perfect. I held the knife up, sharp side down, tip forward, tried a few experimental jabs that would have made Janet Leigh scream her heart out, and then clutched it tightly against my chest.

I put the even flimsier bread knife in the back of my belt in case I needed it later.

Quick and quiet. A sixty-seven-year-old ninja with a goddamn Ginsu knife. I checked the time. Thirty seconds. *Snap, crackle, pop,* went my joints, creaking as I labored to remain still and hidden. Even through the thick apartment wall with its six decades of leaded paint, I heard the loud squeak of the front door swinging open, the hiss as it slowly started to swing closed, and the sudden slam as the gasket Art never replaced gave way. The door slammed and shook the floor beneath my feet.

The sound always seemed to attract Art to his duties as friendly neighborhood bullshitter and time waster. That door summoned him like a chain-smoking genie... usually. But not today. *You stay at the bar today, Art. You're due to win big at the pull-tabs, unless I bribed the wrong afternoon bartender.*

The door to 304 opened outward. It was the last apartment on the left, so the open door ensured no curious neighbors. I took my position in the bathroom and thought to wrap the kitchen towel around my left hand while clutching the butcher knife in my right. The towel would protect my hand, keep him from getting bitey, and maybe soak up some of the blood. There was going to be a lot of blood.

The bread knife, my spare weapon, scraped across my lower back as I turned my body to avoid detection. I ground my teeth against the pain, and I waited.

Clack. The mailbox shut, locked. Up one flight, across the landing, up the next flight, I could hear him open an envelope as he walked. Pressed against the glass of the shower door, I noticed how loud I breathed— felt the first tiny twinges of shortness in the next inhalation of air— then the attack was forgotten as keys jiggled in the lock. Clicked. Turned. The door swung outward and in he trudged.

He was a young man, but carried himself with the weight of age beyond his years, something I'd heard people say about him. I never noticed myself until moments before I killed him.

As I expected, he didn't glance into the bathroom as he flipped on the hall light and the door slammed shut, even though a single look would have shown me staring back in the medicine cabinet mirror. Gym bag with a big notebook and two textbooks— one covered his major, physics, while the other dealt with drama, an arts requirement and a topic on which he gave not two shits. It also contained a Walkman, a spare pack of smokes and some running shoes, and he carried it over one shoulder instead of on his back. Jackass.

Son of a bitch was a few weeks past twenty and had held a fake ID for a year, but so far, the excessive drinking didn't show. But I knew he was hungover today. I'd counted on that, too.

My mental countdown clock reached zero. *Time's up.*

I burst from the bathroom like a goddamn lion. Almost roared, but somehow caught myself. Conscious thought consisted entirely of two words bouncing back and forth: *Quick, quiet. Quiet, quick.*

The younger man managed to turn his head toward me a few inches before I slapped my towel-wrapped left hand over his mouth. He was so surprised he hadn't yet thought to scream, but he remembered a bit too late, after I'd already stuffed the towel into his mouth. Using my leverage and his surprise, I wrenched his head back as he struggled and wailed into the towel, his arms pinned by his own gym bag and the wall. He was strong, but as long as I held him at this angle he had no way to hit back.

I felt my grip beginning to slip and the backpack moving as he tried to wriggle out of the straps. *Now or never.* I raised the knife in my right hand— *that* sure got him screaming into the damned towel— and drew the micro-serrated blade of the bargain-basement Ginsu across the younger man's throat from ear to ear.

Drew. That makes it sound like I just neatly sketched a red line on his Adam's apple and held him close while his life leaked away, gently setting him down in the tub and watching him fade with a 'There, there.' Fact is, I ripped into that throat so aggressively I almost hit vertebrae on the first cut. Half-decapitated him. Blood sprayed up onto the wall, the low ceilings, and the mirror in the bathroom; spattered me as he struggled; reminded me of a Jackson Pollock I used to own. And probably would own again.

He sort of gargled out the rest of his air into the gag. Couldn't have screamed if he'd wanted to, now. Those vocal cords would never function again.

Another few seconds, and the fight went completely out of him, even though I could still feel a fading heartbeat. That'll happen when most of your blood's painting the apartment instead of flowing through your veins. But he was still conscious enough to see the face of his killer reflected in the mirror. I could see it in his eyes, the recognition. Eyes don't lie, in either direction. Despite the years and lines, he knew my face like his own. Which made sense, since it was.

I almost wish he'd been able to talk at that point, even if it had meant I spent the rest of my natural life in prison. It seems like we should've spoken to each other— it's not every day you meet yourself. Here I'd gone straight to the killing. Then again I killed myself and lived to tell about it, too.

Needs must when the devil drives.

II

I noticed the changes kick in a few seconds after the younger me expired, but I have to admit there was a moment or three when I wondered whether I'd been royally ripped off.

Would have served me right. Time travel. It was impossible, right? The entire idea was ludicrous, and if I hadn't been desperate for a few more years of life, I never would have listened to the crazy bastards— even if they did work for me. But I hired them, and they did, in a "Temporal Research Department" squirreled away in a basement of a skyscraper in a city that was definitely not zoned for anything like temporal research. I told them to take initiative, and I am positive I was extremely drunk at the time, but they'd done it.

I had my reasons. I'll get to that. Suffice to say that now, time travel is *not* impossible. And I'd paid some people a whole lot of money to ensure I was the only one who could do it.

Seriously, if one of those brainiacs who actually invented the machine ever tries to use it himself, I will find his earliest known ancestor and wipe his entire family tree off the map. They all know that, which— plus the money— has kept them all loyal, at least as far as I can tell.

Twenty-Me twitched, the heartbeat slowed, inevitably ceased. I stood there shaking like a seizure patient clutching his jacket in one hand as he slumped into it, lifeless. And then the changes I'd been promised arrived right on schedule. They called it 'de-aging.' If I ever intended to let anyone on God's green Earth buy it from me I would come up with something a lot better than that, but damned if it wasn't accurate.

I fought the urge to scream. It wasn't pain, exactly, more like an explosion of nerves and feeling, as if every limb had fallen unpleasantly asleep without going numb. My entire body started to swell, from my groin to my chest to my arms... no, I wasn't *swelling*— de-aging didn't add mass that wasn't there— my skin was *tightening*.

"Holy *Christ*," I said aloud, gaping at my own resurrection in the mirror and letting the twenty-year-old corpse flop into the tub without ceremony. "It's you. Didn't I just kill you?"

They never told me I *had* to do the killing myself. I could have found someone to do it for me. I just didn't trust anyone else to do it right. Some things you should take care of on your own. And yeah, I was selfish. The things I'd created, the business and tech empire that bore my name, and the charities I'd founded helped save the planet Earth, so the planet Earth could excuse the fuck out of me if I took the first damned bite of this apple. And since it was a one-way trip, it would also be the last bite.

All right, maybe an apple wasn't the best metaphor.

It was a mix of luck and ingenuity that made me a multi-billionaire at such a young age. The right observation gets repeated to the right people, a competitor suffers an unfortunate accident— really, a real accident, it wasn't me as far as I know— and the next thing you know I'm sharing magazine covers with Bill Gates and the goddamn president. But you know all about that, and I don't feel like telling it all over again. What wasn't on the magazine covers, not back then, was my company's Temporal Research Department. You remember them. The outfit that broke time travel wide open, once I'd set them to the task with my own initial hypotheses as a starting point.

Thing is, it was never supposed to work. Obviously. Time travel? The shit I've invented in my lifetime, and you really think I thought that was even possible in reality? I only pursued— or rather, had my people pursue— the whole notion as a way to spend some of my billions before my descendants could, the ungrateful shits. Their various mothers had already gotten their share. Let *them* leave something to the bastards. I was spending their inheritance.

Then, a few years in, a few breakthroughs. I started paying more attention to the people in Temporal Research. Before long I wasn't spending out of spite, but on something impossible to see if I could make it possible. Time travel, and with it, immortality. It was a ridiculous idea, but old age was growing boring.

All of which culminated in a newly rejuvenated me, standing in my bloody college apartment astride my own bloody college corpse, and I was the only man alive who knew the future.

To get to that future, though, I had to get rid of the original body without attracting suspicion. There would be no reason to report me missing, so I stuffed my dead self into the refrigerator. I went shopping at a big box home and garden store just outside the city where I wouldn't run into anyone my younger self knew. Over the next two days, I stayed in and worked.

That first time made for some clumsy, dangerous, and frankly disgusting work with a hacksaw and several gallons of acid. One of my first divergences from the timeline would wind up being a few serious plumbing issues Art the building manager would have to deal with someday.

I ran into trouble with the skull, so I stripped it to the bone in acid, wrapped it in a pillowcase, and dumped it down that old central garbage chute no one used anymore. Alas, poor asshole, I knew you too well. Then I changed my second significant piece of personal history— after ruining Art's plumbing— when I moved out of that building a few weeks early.

In the ensuing months, I learned just the kind of man I was. Among other things, I was a horny son of a bitch. I spent that first year of my second chance at life screwing the bejeezus out of every single woman I'd wanted to so much as ask out the first time through. Turns out confidence and secret knowledge of future events make for a winning combination. But I'd be a liar if I said it didn't get a bit... dark. That I didn't go a little crazy, and maybe do some things you don't really need to know about.

Suffice to say I splurged, I got depressed, and I came to deep realizations and realized the realizations were bullshit so went back to screwing for a while. I made a fortune simply gambling— the bigger the wager, the bigger the thrill and more satisfying the victory. I bet on sporting events, I made sound investments and risky ones, and I exploited the living hell out of every single piece of future data I knew. All the while I managed to hit the familiar milestones of the life I'd already led, staying on course to invent time travel or at least hire the geniuses who would. That wasn't optional, all things considered.

Then a few real problems started to crop up, and no matter how many college girls I banged, they weren't going away.

The side investments I'd been unable to resist, the advantages I'd blithely taken, started to have ripple effects. Those ripples must have been rolling out for a long time, but only little ones. The first unexpected difference I really noticed was, of all things, a presidential election, one of the closest the country had ever seen. This time around, the close call led to a recount, and the recount to a court case, only the case got thrown out and the other guy won. It had been a near thing in the first place, sure, but I was positive I remembered it turning out a different way. It had pissed me off too goddamn much.

And when *that* changed, a whole shitload of major events either didn't happen at all, or happened very differently. People like to say it doesn't matter who really runs things, and sure that's true. Some of the shit I wish had never happened still happened. Buildings blew up, people got shot, movies got made and disasters occurred. But other things, things folks don't think much about— appointments, scandals, accidents, personal interactions that never should have occurred— those add up. For example, a particular Austrian-American entertainer never convinced enough backers to help him change the Constitution and get elected president, so the guy who had been my best ally in government when my companies ran into legal trouble ended up in a Hollywood death spiral of action sequels and expensive divorces this time around. I would have to shell out a king's ransom for security and bribes without his help, but my gambling winnings this second time around would cover the expenses.

Temporal elasticity, the eggheads told me, was the weird principle that caused time to stay on more or less the same course provided key milestones were hit. But temporal elasticity or no, this first crack at a second life was a close thing. I pointlessly struggled to figure out what I'd changed. Ridiculous, when you think about it, since I didn't exactly have a way to go back and fix it. At this point no one had invented a time machine yet, even though I was on the way to doing it.

I still made my discoveries, built my inventions, and most of all sold my visionary horseshit. And after a few decades, lo and behold, there I was again receiving a briefing from the same two guys from the same Temporal Research Department. We discussed the potentials of time travel and the de-aging phenomenon. One of them had a moustache this time. He hadn't before. Nevertheless, I couldn't remember his name and his ID badge had flopped around on its lanyard, so he was Moustache. The other was Dr. Treit.

"The quantum replacement may be instantaneous, or it may be gradual. But it is inevitable," Moustache said. "It is inevitable," he repeated, "that the two beings, identical on a quantum level, cannot exist simultaneously."

"How do we find out?" I asked. I'd asked the same question forty-seven years ago by my estimation and run through the same conversation thousands of times in my head, so I knew the answer. It was like relating a scene from a movie you've only seen once, but I could manage.

"We have to send someone back," Dr. Treit said. "An animal specimen will not do. There are too many variables.

The traveler will have to be self-reliant, for the only way to return data to us will be to live the time between then and now."

"Lots of animals live longer than forty-seven years," I said, going off the script before I could catch myself.

"What was that, sir?" Moustache asked.

"Nothing," I said. "Thinking out loud. So why haven't we sent someone back, gentlemen?"

Back on script. Sounded friendly, but there was implied threat in the question: *Why are you bringing this to me?* Jesus, I can really be an asshole, can't I?

"Only that— well, sir, we need permission from the highest levels to— well, to use—"

"What my colleague is trying to say, sir," Dr. Treit said, "is that we have nothing close to the authority to order a human trial in this case. This is not as simple as sending people into the future. That is forward motion through time. That is the direction time wants to go, you see, and we..."

"Speed it up?" I prompted.

"Yes. And when you— that is, a traveler— ventures into the future, you simply become the 'you' of that time. The other you, once you are there, simply ceases to have ever been."

"I know this. But," I replied on cue, "We bring those people back without trouble so long as they don't take their suits off. And there's nothing wrong with changing the future from our perspective. It's the *future*."

"The future, by its very nature, is fungible," Moustache interjected. "In layman's terms, it is like sailing on a wide, gently flowing river at the point the delta forms. As long as you turn around before you enter the ocean— the future we cannot predict algorithmically— it is almost as simple to move upstream as it is down, when the water is so wide the current is slow. But the past, the past is a series of straight points."

"A line," I said, and mentally added, *Duh. Brilliant,*

asshole. Listen for once. You're smart— smart enough to hire people smarter than you.

"Er, yes— a line," Moustache said. "But also a slope. And a tube. And— well, to complete our analogy, sir, if the future is a broad river delta of possibilities, the past is a water slide, and one does not easily climb back up a water slide. The only solution is to launch the traveler back up the chute with great force and hope that he reaches the top. The beginning, in terms of temporal causality."

I was growing impatient, and went off script again just to hurry things along. I released a practiced sigh, a small, efficient sound that I'd learned long ago could stop an underling— and though these fellows were certainly geniuses, they were still sure as hell underlings— in his tracks. I leaned back in my chair and made a show of staring for a full seven seconds at the setting sun from my expansive penthouse office window. Then I focused on the two men like a laser. I think Moustache even jumped a little.

"Gentlemen," I said. "I'll do it. I will launch myself up your water slide of time."

"But— but *sir*," Dr. Treit said. "You don't understand. This is what we are trying to tell you. It's completely untested on anything more complex than a slime mold! Surely, we can't risk you, of all people. It's unthinkable."

"Don't kiss my ass, doctor," I replied, and then threw in a little something new that I wished I'd said the first time I lived through this conversation. "I can't ask someone else to take the risk."

I grimaced at the thought of how another forty-seven years of living had taken a toll on this body too, even if I had quit smoking a lot earlier this second time around. I reverted to the original script of this conversation, best as I could remember it. "This body goes away, and I become young, vital me again."

"Not exactly," Moustache said, squirming a little in his seat. There was a look on Moustache's face that gave me pause. For a second— just a second— I wanted to call the whole thing off. Live my years out until I reached the ripe old mental age of one hundred and fourteen while still within the body of a sixty-seven-year-old. Relatively speaking, I was just entering middle age.

Moustache cleared his throat. I'd been staring at his forehead while thinking my deep, existential time traveling thoughts. Still had a part to play. No turning back now. And nothing to worry about. I'd proven that to myself the first time around. Finally, I put a finger to my temple as if I'd been thinking on his words intently the entire time.

"'Not exactly'... how?" I asked, with appropriate skepticism.

"It may... that is, it *could* cause your death," Dr. Treit said. "We believe— though we have not unequivocally proven— that the mind of the chronologically more advanced specimen is the one that survives, but we have no way—"

"You think the mind of the older me will be the winner," I said. "So that means I get a new body just by showing up. Odds are he'll just disappear. But if he doesn't what are my options, Dr. Treit?"

I waited. *Go ahead, Treit,* I thought. *Tell me. I'll have to* kill *the other me.* He had called it 'suicidal homicide.' It depended on two people being in the same point on the timeline and trying to occupy the same exact quantum state. Yep, we all have one of those, the good doctor told me, and it's unique. Two unique things existing at the same time is something the universe doesn't like, it seems. Treit had then gone on to explain how extinguishing the literal spark of life— shutting down bioelectric activity in the brain— was enough of a change in the quantum state that it allowed, in theory, the living copy to go native. Whichever version is left standing, in other words, physically becomes the version from that point in the timeline. A sixty-seven-year-old who met his twenty-year-old self and somehow caused the death of the twenty-year-old would *become* the twenty-year-old on a quantum level.

I almost jumped ahead in my mental script to tell the doctor it sounded like magic when I realized he still hadn't said a thing. *Come on,* I thought, *you laughed when you said it.* 'Suicidal homicide.' We all three of us laughed, in fact, because it was such a ridiculous thing to say. To be honest I didn't even entirely understand it the first time around. But goddamn it, Treit was exactly right. I was living proof, though I sure as hell couldn't tell him that.

Go on. Say it.

"Something I call 'homicidal suicide,' sir," Treit said.

I forgot to laugh and slapped him instead. I get slappy when surprised. Ask anyone.

I apologized, hoping I hadn't gotten the immediate timeline too far off-track again. Yet inwardly I was concerned. What if something else was different? What if some numbers and equations had been swapped as well, and the machine didn't work correctly?

Then again... the machine looked right. I'd had it inspected. Now to see if it was not just a time machine, but an immortality machine.

I stood and launched into the words that would be included in Dr. Treit's best-selling nonfiction book about the invention of time travel and the disappearance of the man who made it all possible. "I've made up my mind. I'm going back up that water slide, gentlemen. I'm going to find out whether this works or not. I'll leave a note— something— we'll figure out a way to tell if I've made it. If I do, I get an extra thirty-seven years. If I don't, well, what have I lost?"

"The rest of your life?" said Moustache.

"Ah, but Doctor," I said, repeating my words I remembered so well, "If what you're telling me is correct, the rest of my life is only just beginning."

III

It was a lot trickier to murder a *thirty*-year-old wunderkind on the verge of several scientific breakthroughs that would change the world than it was to take out 'Twenty-Me,' especially when I knew this wunderkind was already a time traveler. He was almost as much *me* as I was, so I couldn't count on the flexibility I had before. Twenty-Me was boring as hell, Thirty-Me was a busy man.

As it turned out my thirtieth birthday, the trip to Hawaii, was about the only time it would work. I wasn't so extravagant then— the business was only just starting to come together, so even though the promise of my research had already paid off well enough to afford a month's house rental on the north shore of Kauai, I hadn't even bought my first jet. More to the point, I had money, but no entourage traveling with me yet. Even though this version of me was living through things a second time, he still took extra care not to break the timeline.

After I packed the cash and contemporary materials to ease my way round the world— or at least from Seattle to Kauai in the late twentieth century— I headed back as early as I dared. Drs. Treit and Stein (Moustache's ID badge had finally flipped back around) warned me that seventy-two hours was the best I could hope for before some sort of 'catastrophic temporal incident' happened if I didn't kill the younger me.

This second arrival was less accurate than the first, and a lot less pleasant. Treit and Stein nailed the time of arrival to the millisecond, but the three-dimensional coordinates were trickier to manage. Later I'd get them to work on that, but this was still early in my lives yet.

Fortunately the water wasn't deep or far from the beach. I kept my cool, swam straight upward, and when I broke the surface, no one noticed an extra bodysurfer on the incoming tide. When I waded out of the ocean, no one gave a second glance to another beach bum coming back to dry land. Even my dress slacks, white shirt, and tie didn't raise any questions from strangers. Clearly I wasn't the first, or they didn't care, or both.

I found Thirty-Me on a familiar beach, just past noon and well into his sixth Kahlua and second joint of the day. Looking at this version of thirty-year-old-me, this idiot who was already a time traveler but had yet to fuck things up, I vividly remembered how careful I'd been the second time around to get everything the same as before.

This day was a few months after that presidential election let me know about the botched timeline, and Thirty-Me was already having doubts. On vacation alone, the first without his wife of two years (it would not be the last, and she'd get her share of my fortune in another couple of years on her way out the door). For the second time, this time traveling jerk found himself drinking like a fish, screwing like a teenager (Viagra! Not just for the *physically* ancient anymore!) and flipping a rental Ford Mustang into a goddamn Kauai horse ranch, of all places. Getting *that* right the second time around hadn't been fun, though he walked away from it without a scratch just like before. Paid off the people who needed paying off while standing amid the broken pieces of horses and car.

This time I had arrived about three days after he'd redone that eventful stretch of vacation. No way in hell was I going through that accident thrice. That gave me a couple of days to get the job done.

First I picked up some sunscreen and more appropriate beachwear. With expertly forged paperwork and credit I rented a beach house not far from the one I'd rented both times I was thirty, then I hit the beach and headed toward Thirty-Me's rental. I ordered in, raided the liquor cabinet with impunity. The next day I bought a small .22 pistol from a shop that would make sure there was no record of the purchase for an added gratuity.

It's true what people who have been shot say. You don't hear the blast, you only feel the bullet. What they don't say is that you don't hear the shot because the bullet gets there first, and the bullet hurts like a thousand jagged rusty blades stabbing you in the same place at the same time while someone pours lemon juice into the wound.

So yeah, the sound of the shot kind of gets lost in the fray. But then there's the realization: *Jesus fucking Christ I just got shot*. I dropped to my knees and turned, clumsily, to see who had shot me.

"The tree line," said Thirty-Me from the wicker lounge chair. He'd barely reacted. "But you'll never hit him with that thing. Trust me, I've seen this part."

I looked at the .22 in my hand. Almost forgot it was there. The gun dropped from my grip with a soft thud into the dry sand. Dry for now, but already turning red. Thirty-me stood up and stomped toward me just as my legs gave out.

IV

I got up from the wicker chair. The fat, old, balding me raised a hand like he was going to try and reach me, even though he was more than ten feet away. "Good god, was I really as stupid as this?" I asked the physically elderly version of myself.

"You couldn't," old, dying me managed. Sixty-seven-me. "Know, you couldn't know..." The words were wheezes crushed from starving lungs. "You couldn't. Know. I. Didn't. Know."

"No, you did not, old man," I said. "And the you you *think* I am is not the you I *know* I am. You know, I sound like an asshole when I use pronouns. That happen to you? It will. Or won't. I don't know, really. This is going to be interesting finding out."

He was fading fast. I felt fine. Better than fine, in fact. Thank you, stretchiness of time. I crouched over Sixty-Seven-Me when he tipped over sideways and began to shiver. "How?" the old man whispered in my ear. Or maybe I imagined he asked. I answered regardless.

"I'm not *that* you, dumbass. Not the you I thought I was.

The first traveler," I said, pushing myself back to my feet. "I'm the... well, I've lost count really. Glad to meet you, like always." The old man let me pull him back up to his knees. When I saw he wasn't going to tip over again, I reached to the small of my back and drew a much larger handgun from the belt under my trunks. Affixed to the barrel was an utterly illegal suppressor. I took aim at old-me's forehead.

"You have no idea how many times I've done this. How many times I went back, further and further, just to change things again. To fix them because some jackass gets hold of a stray nuke thanks to the outcome of a boxing match I changed. Or because some goddamn apocalyptic disease ends up killing the Eastern Seaboard thanks to a strain of future flu I unintentionally brought back. Or some fundamentalist whack job manages to assassinate someone thanks to me tipping a Ukrainian stripper to give him a handjob. But you... you were just *bored,* so you became a murderer. Waited a long time to meet you, you son of a bitch. You deserve this more than any of us."

The older me's eyes widened as his hand lowered.

"But you're. Me," the second traveler wheezed. His sixty-seven-year-old frame began to slump.

"No shit," I said. "I'm *all* of us. Every single me. And I'm going to fix it all, even if I have to kill every last one of me."

I took a breath, squeezed the trigger, and shot my older self right between the eyes. His head jerked back with the impact and then ricocheted forward when the bullet exited the back of his head with a cloud of red and gray mist and chunks of heavier matter. My sixty-seven-year-old body flopped over and twitched like a dying fish for a few minutes, then finally went still.

Then the old man's memories, the ones that diverged from my own, appeared unbidden in my mind in a flash of images that made me momentarily dizzy, but I soon regained my footing. I walked over to the corpse and patted down the second traveler's pockets. He was carrying a lot of cash, but no identification. I waved toward the tree line to a man nearly identical to the corpse on the beach, but a decade or so older, stooped and white-haired.

"Thanks for the warning," I said. "I'm ready now."

"You sure?" The elderly me asked. "This— we don't know for sure. Two time machines—"

"Two time travelers," I replied. "It was the only way to surprise me."

"Smart kid," he said.

"Kid? I don't look it, but I'm older than you. Which one were you again?"

"Not quite smart enough, though," the elderly version of me said as he raised the rifle, the one he'd used to put a bullet in Sixty-Seven-Me a few minutes earlier.

I realized just before he fired that I didn't remember doing that. Turns out you really can lie to yourself. I wasn't *all* of us after all.

V

I was. I was all of us, all of me, the last of the bunch and one smart bastard. I was the one who did the worst thing you could do to yourself, and I paid for it too. Then I went off-script. *Way* off-script.

Thirty-me— *this version* of Thirty-Me— thought he was avenging humanity on the bad man he'd been, but he didn't know the half of it. When he later had reached that magic age— golden sixty-seven— he, *I,* realized what I was letting go to waste. Not just for me, but for the world. I wasn't just that asshole who was lucky enough to hire some fellows who invented time travel, not anymore. I had lived for a very long time, jumping back earlier and earlier from age thirty and twenty. In every lifetime my entire fortune sprang from some lucky timing and clever innovations early on, leaving me to try different variations on sitting back to let my people do all the work. I hadn't applied myself, even though I knew more about everything than anyone who ever lived, because I had always feared losing my hard-won immortality.

I wasn't afraid of that anymore. To hell with the old timelines. I reckoned it was time I made a new one, with a mind hundreds, thousands of years old. I was the smartest man who ever lived, and I owed it to myself, to humanity, not to let myself die. That was when it occurred to me I already knew more than enough to make a new time machine, as many new time machines as I wanted, without the help of Treit and Stein or the Temporal Research Department.

That's how I ended up with three— the two the man I'd just killed knew about, and the extra one I had just used to betray and murder him. I knew the physics of it like I knew the back of my hand, and had seen so many working variations of the concept I could probably have built one out of a flashlight and a stick of gum, given enough time.

So there I was, a version of Thirty-Me dead at my feet, his face a mask of surprise. As he breathed his last, I took a deep breath of my own. Seconds later de-aging kicked in, and what was left of his mind and thoughts became mine.

With the renewed strength of a thirty-year-old, I hauled the body over one shoulder and back into the house. I had rented a place with an extremely large tub, and was pretty sure I could find someone who would deliver a few barrels of hydrochloric acid without making a thing out of it.

"It's been fun, Thirty-Me-Too," I told the corpse as I hacked off each piece and dropped it gently— no need for dangerous splash-back— into the acid. "But you know you're just a pit stop on this trip. Well, you know now. Didn't know before, did you?"

The corpse stubbornly refused to reply, but he was down to most of a torso and a head. I wouldn't have replied either.

"Suit yourself. I'll take care of it." And another me boiled and sizzled in the corrosive bath.

VI

The next morning I went back to Seattle and found my original time machine right where Treit and Stein had built it. Getting past security wasn't an issue. I was gone before the good Drs. Treit or Stein even noticed I'd activated the machine. They never missed their lunchtime D&D game. One of the true consistencies of the timeline, I assure you. That also meant they wouldn't notice I'd programmed the machine's power systems to overload and shut down the fail-safes. With luck and a good alarm system, no one would die— and without me around, I doubted the company would have any reason to waste tremendous resources developing any more time machines.

This time I arrived at the end of a quiet dirt road, and damn me if I hadn't stuck the landing— no dips in the nearby lake because Stein's assistant spilled coffee on the geospatial stabilizer circuit, no dropping into a tree because Treit thought a 7 was a 2. Feet on dirt. I should've been operating my own equipment all along.

The moon wasn't too bright and I was grateful. It was a sleepy little mountain community amid a thick forest of evergreens, its mostly rural residents making a living logging or working at the lumber mills. The night was cold and brisk. I wished I'd brought a jacket but at least I was wearing a dark suit that wouldn't stand out. I didn't count on much traffic, but even so, I knew I should get off the road immediately. My safe landing area was also very exposed, and a man my age walking down this particular road at this time of night would, at the very least, be greeted by someone driving home. More likely he'd be challenged, threatened, even shot at. I kept to the woods and avoided the few dogs that barked and bayed as I slipped past.

The closest call I had was at my destination. An old man— who was not me, I hasten to add— stepped out onto his porch and flicked on an electric porch light. The porch light made me miss the flashlight in his hand, and the beam flashed across me before I could take cover.

"Who's out there?" the man called as I nevertheless dove into the nearest hiding place I could find, a thicket of blackberry bushes overgrowing a ditch. "I will shoot you if you do not get off my property!"

So far, so good, the man was still on his porch. The bird rifle he carried hung open, as if he'd been in the process of loading when he saw me in his flashlight beam. He had never been a man who would threaten with a gun when yelling would do. The noisy dogs in the area were lucky in that regard.

I waited for him to continue. I hadn't heard that voice in a long time.

"You better be gone. I am calling the police, and if you ain't gone when they get here, you're going to jail!"

No, but I'll be going all the same. Just get back inside. As if he could read my urgent thoughts, the old man took one last look, and finally invoked the name of one of his many local nemeses. "Hell. Must have been one of them Jacobson kids." He scratched the dog's ear. "Go on inside, Duffer." The dog responded by bolting off into the woods to chase shadows and rabbits, as usual. With a chuckle and a shake of his head, the old man went back inside the house and locked the door. He left the electric porch light burning.

It wasn't that bright to begin with, but the angle at which the lone, unadorned light hung from the aging red and blue wires made it easy for me to slip around the patch of light and within reach of the bulb. From my pocket, I pulled a gruesome trophy I'd collected from a nearby pasture earlier that day— a freshly strangled garter snake about a foot long. Eyeing the patches where the copper wiring above the bulb was visible in the dim orange light, I swung the snake's small corpse across the wires and let go as a jolt of electricity shot down the serpent's spine. It ignited with a flash of green flame just as the light bulb shattered. The burning snake dropped onto the dry blankets the dog slept on when the old man locked her outside.

To be safe, I took one final, long drag on my last cigarette— for now— and flung it onto the stack of old newspapers next to the woodpile. My father used the newspapers
for kindling when starting fires. As I turned and ran back
into the woods, I heard a baby's voice wail from the upper
story of the small brown house, and the terrified shouts of
my parents, burning alive as they tried in vain to save their
only son.

VII

So I want to say thank you for the cake. It's really a nice
one. There's no way you could possibly put enough candles on it, and for appearance's sake I understand why you
only put on five. As far as you know, that's how old I am.
Well, as far as you *knew*. Cat's out of the bag now, if you're
actually paying attention to what I'm saying and not just
nodding along while you watch game shows and collect a
check from the state to keep me alive long enough to be
passed on to the next foster parent.

Does not look like you are paying attention, though,
and that's fine. You needn't engage me in any kind of
grand debate. I'm not quite ready to start driving, or get
a job, or anything like that yet. But I won't trouble you for
long. I'll hang around in the system until I can plausibly
depart, and then I am off like a dirty shirt.

And why not? I'm the goddamn miracle baby. Found
alive and naked, aged three months, crawling down the
side of a road leading from a house that burned to the
ground in less than half an hour. My dear parents the vic-
tims of a modern scourge, faulty wiring. The foolish old
man had doomed his entire family by using an unadorned
light bulb for a porch light. The casing around the wires
dried and cracked, you see, until something— probably a
bug, but maybe a really unlucky squirrel— happened to

help bring a couple of those wires into contact, sparking that dried-out casing to catch fire. The real tragedy was how the parents died. Front porch ablaze and the back door had been padlocked.

From the look of things, no one had been able to find the key. Folks suspected foul play until someone suggested the old man had starting padlocking that door pending the replacement of a doorknob he never managed to change. That seemed plausible. The first firefighter to suggest it wasn't sure where he'd heard the idea. He certainly didn't hear it from the miracle baby.

The real miracle was how the baby came to arrive outside the house without so much as a smudge of ash on his person. People ultimately figured the old man, if not the missus, had managed to push the lad out an upper story window wrapped in a blanket that saved his life. Others swore it must have been a guardian angel. Funny thing, though, was no one ever did say they *saw* the baby come out through that window.

No one ever looked for incinerated remains in the crib with the baby safe. No one shed any tears for little zero-me, who died so that I might live again from the very beginning. No one else heard the screams I heard, fresh from the future, as flames consumed the house.

Me, I'll never stop hearing them, but needs must when the devil drives.

Author's Note: Cory J. Herndon

The first time travel story I remember obsessing over as a child was, not surprisingly, a *Star Trek* story, an animated D.C. Fontana-written episode from the 1970s called "Yesteryear." In it Mr. Spock uses the time donut from the Joan Collins episode to go back and help his younger self through some rough adolescent business. I frequently revisited the tale via worn Viewmaster discs that adapted the episode into a few dozen frames of bold color action and green Vulcan bear-cats. I eventually found a prose version adapted by Alan Dean Foster, but that Viewmaster disc remained my time machine.

As a nerdy kid who spent his time in books (or Viewmasters) it was an attractive idea, going back and correcting your life. Saving yourself from bullies, helping young you through a loss, giving your parents a nudge to make them treat you differently. I'm also a writer, so naturally I wanted to go back and replace my poorly edited younger selves with my more knowledgeable future self. While I'd eventually grow more familiar with this and other time travel tropes, the idea of self-interaction, literal conflict with one's self, and the chance to make an earlier self a better or happier person remained the most intriguing type of time travel tale for me.

I think about time travel, both as a concept and as a sub-sub-genre of fiction, probably more than is healthy. The idea of going back and fixing mistakes comes naturally to a writer. Doing so with reality itself? Who wouldn't want to do that?

A Thousand Stitches

Kate Jonez

'It was not only pathetic, it was ludicrous,' a writer, whose name I forget, said about his father's tailor shop.

That's a pretty apt description of the situation in the back room at Malley's Dry Cleaners. I'm not going to be here much longer which is a good thing because I'd be forced to take desperate measures if this situation wasn't temporary. I'm just working until I save up enough to move to New York.

Judy says we used to get all different kinds of work. She says we even used to get orders to make suits and evening gowns. That would be so sweet. I would love to design and make something like that. I'd love to have a job where I could use my talent. Why someone would go to a tailor shop in the back room at Malley's Cleaners to get their evening gown made, I don't know, but that's what Judy says.

Since I've been here, what we mostly get is wedding dresses. Sometimes we replace a zipper or put new buttons on a dress shirt but the vast majority of the work is taking the feathers, sequins, or jewels off the wedding gowns so they can be cleaned then sewing all the stuff back on once they're done. Even though there are a million colors in the world, every single one of the princess bridal dresses are white. We have a whole separate rack just for white thread. The women in this town don't have a speck of imagination. Nobody here does. I can't wait to leave.

My wedding dress, not that I'd ever want one, but if I

did, my dress would be hurricane-sky yellow or pumpkin orange. Something that shows that I'm not just another cow in the herd. Judy says hers was ruby red. I guess Judy was married once. I have trouble imagining that.

Even after they've been cleaned, the wedding dresses smell faintly of the expensive perfume the bride bought for her special day and never wore again. A surprising number of them have the lingering scent of vomit and sex. 'Special day' smells I guess. The work is the essence of meaningless. These dresses will be stashed away in attics or cedar trunks never to be worn again. I feel like I'm sewing up shrouds except my work doesn't even get to clothe a corpse. It just gets buried.

I remove the last of the seed pearls from a bodice and place them in a baby food jar. I sit cross-legged on my bench because that's how tailors are supposed to sit. Judy says it's going to twist my spine and make me a cripple before I'm forty. Judy always says things like that. I'm not exactly sure where she gets her information. And even if it is true, forty is a long way away. I'll probably never even make it that far. My mom doesn't think I'll make it to middle-age. She thinks I need to change my ways. She might be right.

I like doing things the traditional way. It makes me feel authentic. Sewing is the only real thing left. Writers write on computers and singers' voices are auto-tuned. Movies are full of fake special effects. Even photographers manipulate images so much they don't have anything to do with what the eye actually sees. Sewing is the only real thing left. There's no way to do it electronically. It's honest and true. That's a good thing.

A wisp of menthol smoke wafts out of the ladies room that only Judy and I use. The water runs a really long time, then the door under the sink slams shut. I'm pretty sure Judy stashed her pillow and comforter under there. The hiss of hair spray from a can filters through the hum of dry cleaning machines and the mechanical rumble of the overhead racks in the rest of the store.

She's been in there for several hours, ever since I got to work this morning. Judy has been pushing the boundaries for months, staying in the ladies room longer each day. No one has noticed yet. Or maybe they look the other way because she's worked here so long. I don't mind. Sometimes I work extra fast so she won't have to work so hard to catch up. Not that she would. She covers for me, too, when I need a nap.

The dresses we are working on fill the racks and surround our little enclosure like puffy, bloated dancers in a chorus line. Something about the way air circulates through Malley's makes the fabric swish ever so slightly, as if someone on the other side has brushed their hand along them. It's creepy when we come in early or stay late and no one else is in the building. It's creepy all the time, actually.

Judy's cigarette hits the water in the toilet with a satisfying sizzle. She steps out of the ladies' room with every loop and wave of her silver hair in exactly the right spot. Her lipstick is perfect. It doesn't bleed into the creases around her lips like I've seen on some old ladies. I wish I had the confidence to wear the shades of red she does. She smooths her leopard print dress over her angular hips and pushes her ruffled cuffs up to her elbows. Then she sits in her chair in front of the dusty old treadle machine that hasn't been used for as long as I've been here. Judy's eyes look puffy. Her skin seems a little gray under her make-up. I hope she's not sick. She'd never admit it if she was.

"He's going to catch you smoking." I say.

Judy pulls an enormous mound of crinoline and white silk onto her lap. For a moment it seems as if it might swallow her, but with a no-nonsense air she pushes the glasses hanging around her neck up onto her nose and crushes the unruly dress into submission.

"The old man didn't care if we smoke, why should he?" She punctuates her words with a jab of the tiny golden scissors she uses to snip especially tight stitches.

I shrug. "He's an idiot."

"Now there's an understatement. That brat better watch his step around me, or I'll bring the old man back from the other side to give him a stern 'how do you do.'" Judy's laugh is raspy as a fine tooth saw and always seems about to decay into a fit of coughing. It exactly captures her sense of humor. Harsh and always in danger of becoming something more sinister. That's a good thing. More people should laugh in a dangerous way.

"Can you do that?" I tag the dress I was working on and put it in the bin for the tumblers. "Can you bring him back? You know, summon him?" I'm not sure if I believe in ghosts but it would be absolutely perfect if they were real. I'll believe it when I see it.

"I've never tried." Judy's scissors make little 'tic, tic, tic' sounds as she removes stitches. "But if anyone could raise that man from the dead, I'd be the one who could do it." Judy winks at me to make sure I don't miss the double entendre.

The dresses sway. The petticoats rustle. The hairs on my arms prickle as a gust of cold air blows over me.

I let my mouth fall open in mock surprise. "You had an affair with the boss."

"The idea that *he* was the boss might not stand up to scrutiny." Judy laughed her dangerous laugh.

"But he was married."

"Minor detail."

Judy is so completely awesome. I hope I have a life like hers. I will, I know it, once I get to New York.

"Does Ron know?"

"Does Ron know what?" Ron pushes a clothing cart piled high with garments through a gap between the racks of swaying dresses.

I snap my mouth shut and wait for my heart to stop pounding. I hate when Ron sneaks up on us.

"Is that the same dress you've been working on for the

last three days?" He glares at the pile of silk and crinoline piled on the treadle machine.

Judy looks over the top of her glasses. If she had laser vision, she would have burned a hole right through the spot where Ron's too-narrow tie knots around his over long neck.

"Did you not get my email?"

Ron smells faintly of lighter fluid mixed with rotten banana. It's from the dipropylene glycol he used to replace the percloroethylene his father preferred. To be fair Perc is not a good cleaning solvent. It was the first carcinogen ever identified by the CDC. But this new stuff has to be even worse. Ron worries about fire hazards constantly. It's a good thing since the new chemical is probably as flammable as it smells. By the strength of his pungent aroma, it would seem like he climbs right in the machines and tumbles around with the clothes.

"Well?"

"I don't have email," I say. I'm supposed to get email on my phone and tell Judy, but I never remember to charge it. I'm not really into electronic communication anyway.

"I thought we solved this." Ron says. He's trying to hold his body like he's in charge. Maybe he read a self-help book about body language. The effect is comic, like Othello performed in extra-amateur community theater. It's clear that even though he's trying not to show it he's intimidated by Judy.

Judy releases the dress and its crinolines expand and swallow up the treadle machine.

"Why aren't these garments logged?" Ron grips the handle of the cart and draws his lips into a thin line. He speaks in what I can tell he intends to be a forceful tone.

Even though Judy's stooped over a little because she's old, she's easily four inches taller than Ron. That can't help his body language any. She jiggles the cord on the hot plate. It crackles a little and she places the kettle on it.

"You can't have that back here." His voice wavers like

he had to gather his courage to speak at all as he points at the hot plate. He looks at me like I'm the one making tea.

"The old man authorized it back when you were in grade school."

"Get rid of it." Ron's neck and cheeks turn red. "Today."

Judy folds her arms and steps between Ron and the hot plate. "We'll just have to take it up with the old man, won't we?"

Ron clenches his teeth. Among the racks of rainbow-hued spools of thread, baskets of fabric scraps, teetering boxes, jars of buttons and bags stuffed with spare doodads and dangles (as Judy calls them), he is drained of all color like a pencil sketch. Ron is out of his element in our exploded Barbie Dream house that robins have made into a nest. As crowded and cluttered as it is, I like our little work space. It may look like a mess, but we can find things. My studio in New York, when I get one, is going to be just like this only bigger.

"Why aren't you doing your work? We've got people waiting."

"I am." I say, waving my hand at the racks of wedding dresses. If we ever run out of work from the racks, there's a stack of fancy dress store boxes stuffed with even more.

"Not the bridals, Laura Beatty." Ron's voice squeaks with the intensity of his emotion. "You have to read your email."

Everyone calls me by my first and last name like it's one word. I can't even remember when it started. I used to hate it, but I don't anymore. I'm like the opposite of Beyoncé.

"Well what then. I don't know what you want."

Ron's sigh is as loud as the explosion of steam from the presser.

"The tailor shop needs to start pulling its weight. It needs to generate more business."

"People don't tailor their clothes the way they used to do." Judy touches the tea kettle to see if it's hot. It must not be yet. Some tea would be nice. It would also be nice if Ron would go back to whatever he was doing before.

"New policy." Ron folds his arms just like Judy. He sets his jaw. He's thought about how he's going to say this. He probably practiced in the mirror. "Zippers, buttons and hems are same day service."

"What!" Judy's eyes flash with anger. She stomps her foot. "That's as idiotic as you are."

"You're already behind." Ron shoves the cart in my direction as though he didn't even hear Judy call him idiotic. "Focus. This has to be done by 5 p.m."

"Or what?" Judy's question is more of a threat.

"All this?" I stare at the mountain of jeans with pink ribbons threaded through their button holes to mark broken zippers; slacks and skirts pinned up with green headed pins; and shirts with yellow flags safety-pinned where they need a button. "This is too much for one day."

"One basket equals one day's pay." Ron's smug little eyes narrow to self-satisfied slits.

"You can't do that." I say but a tremble works its way up from my hands to my face because I don't have any power. None at all. Without this job, I'll never make it to New York.

I should never have bought those new winter boots. Or other things that I'm not going to beat myself up about. Everybody messes up sometimes. My savings are not even close to where they should be.

The kettle vibrates on the hot plate as the water begins to boil. "You can't pay sweatshop wages." Judy says. "Not in this day and age."

"That's right." Tears feel like they're about to roll down my cheeks. This is not the time for tears. "It's illegal."

Ron's smug little smirk grows into a full-blown grin. "Have your lawyer call me." He tries to hold my gaze like he's tough but he looks away first. To hide his failure, he pushes aside the poof of the wedding dresses and marches down the aisle in the direction of the front counter.

"That little weasel." Judy takes two teacups and a tin of Earl Gray from the shelf. "Don't worry about him."

I frantically paw through the basket of work. "There's more here than we can do in *two* days. Even if we work faster than we ever have before, there's no way we can get it done." I jerk open the drawer where we keep the zippers and dig through them looking for a match. "What if we have to order supplies!" Panic is rising up in me and squeezing my throat closed. I'm more aware than ever before of the toxic dry cleaning fumes. I want to go outside to breathe some regular air, but I don't have time.

"A thousand stitches, right?" I try to smile at Judy but my face feels twitchy and wrong. I grab the button tin. It slips from my hands. Buttons scatter, bouncing and rolling in every direction. I fall to my knees.

"Leave that." Judy says holding out a teacup. "Sit."

"But..."

"Sit."

I take the tea and sit on my tailor's bench. My mind races as it enumerates all the little tasks that fill the basket. "He can't get away with this."

"He'll get away with it," Judy says, "over my dead body."

I don't know where she gets her confidence, but she says it with such conviction I almost believe her.

"Drink up."

I take a sip of the tea. I don't really like it. It tastes more flowery than ordinary tea because the tin has been stored next to the perfume-soaked wedding gowns for so long. The essence of long gone and stored away 'special days' floats like a skin of grease on my tea.

"Drink it down."

I take another sip.

"All of it." Judy watches as I drain my cup. She takes it from me and tips the tea leaves into the saucer.

Her chair squeals as she slides it across the floor and wedges it next to my bench. She peers over the top of her glasses as she studies the leaves. "Uh huh. Just what I thought." She puts the saucer under my nose. "See that?"

I see a bunch of soggy tea leaves that smell even more

sickly than they did in my cup. "I guess."

The whites of Judy's eyeballs have a yellowish tinge. Maybe it's because she's tired. Her breath smells odd too, like spoiled fruit.

"Then it's settled." Judy places the saucer on the edge of my bench.

"What is?"

"You're going to New York."

"Is that what the tea leaves said?" I start to feel a little better like maybe there is a glimmer of hope after all. "I've been so worried I won't have enough—"

Judy grabs her big purse with all of the pockets and drags it onto her lap. She digs around inside. She frowns as if she can't find what she's looking for. "I remember now. It's in the drawer." She points.

I squat down to inspect the contents of the drawer. It's where we keep our invoices and order forms. I riffle through the paperwork.

"There. That's it."

I pull out a manila envelope closed with a rubber band.

"What is it?"

"Open it."

I unwind the elastic and reach my hand inside. Money. A lot of it. "What—"

"You're going to New York." Judy stands up fast like she's in a hurry to be somewhere. "Today." She grabs the corner of the sewing machine table to steady herself. "That's three thousand dollars. Enough to get you started. This is your chance."

Why is she doing this? Judy won't even loan me money for a soda. She is the definition of tight with a dollar.

"I can't take this." I say, but I know I can. She wouldn't offer it to me if she didn't want me to take it. With this much money, I can pay all the incidental fees that my student loan doesn't cover. I can find a place to live. I can be enrolled in Parsons School for Design by the spring semester.

Judy doesn't bother to argue with me. She knows I'm

going to go. She knows I want this more than anything ever.

"You can take that money, all of it. No strings attached except one."

I clutch the envelope a little tighter than is probably polite.

"You have to go now."

I blink at her. "You mean right now? This minute?"

"Yes."

I open my mouth to argue but I don't. There is no reason not to walk outside and take the bus to the train station. Not one single reason. I'm really going to go. Today.

"You're going to do fine. Remember it takes a thousand stitches to make one dollar. Don't waste any more stitches. Use yours to make the prettiest dresses New York has ever seen."

"Why don't you come with—"

"You'll need a winter coat." Judy grabs her nubby wool jacket with the real fox collar off the hanger. She drapes it around my shoulders. "Make me proud of you, Laura Beatty."

Judy never says she expects me to fail. She's seen me screw up just like everybody else has but she never tells me I drink too much or I stay out too late and take crazy chances. She always talks to me like the things I dream are already real. How am I going to leave her behind?

"What are you going to do?" I ask. I wish I wasn't crying but there's nothing I can do to stop it.

Judy smiles a smile that's as dangerous as her laugh. "I'm going to take a nap." She turns away, kicks off her shoes in the middle of the floor and walks into the ladies room. The door closes with a delicate click. I breathe in the stale perfume and chemical smell of Malley's one last time. The scent of menthol cigarettes drifts from under the ladies room door.

~

My bus pulls into Port Authority at 5 a.m. This is the time

I get up most days so I can get to Malley's by six. This time of year it's dark this early. Not here, though. More than half an hour ago the lights of Manhattan changed the velvet black tapestry of the night sky to the color of neon dusk. My heart races as I step off the train and into the river of early commuters. I think about pinching myself. I am here. Against all the odds, I am here.

The ring of an old fashioned telephone startles me. I guess I remembered to charge it for once. I reach into my pocket and pull it out. "Hello."

"Laura Beatty, oh my god. I've been so worried."

"What's wrong, Mom?"

"I've been calling you for hours. Why haven't you answered your phone? I've been worried sick." Her voice is shaky like when I was a kid and she found me at the bottom of the stairs with a broken arm. Her voice sounds far away. Even farther away than it really is, like I'm talking to her through a portal to a different time.

"I'm fine. Why wouldn't I be?"

"There was a fire at Malley's. The whole place burned to the ground. Nobody knew where you were."

"Oh no. Was anyone hurt?"

I can't believe that Malley's is gone. Now I don't even have the option to fail. I don't have anywhere to go back to.

"Everyone got out in time, except no one could find you."

"I'm here. I'm fine."

I let the flow of the crowd push me onto 42nd St.

"Where's Judy? Did she get out in time?"

"Not that again, Laura Beatty." Mom sighs like she caught me stealing from her liquor cabinet again. "I thought we decided with the doctor, it isn't healthy to talk about these things as though they are real."

My mother has no idea, *no idea*, what's real or what's not. By *these things* she means delusions that I do not have. The doctor was her idea. Judy says you can learn a lot about what's wrong with a person by watching what they try to make other people do. My mom would be a lot better off if she'd just admit *she's* the one with the problem.

She is totally without spirituality.

"Okay, Mom. But *no one* was hurt right?"

"That's right." My mom pauses to inhale. I can tell she's gathering steam for a lecture.

"I've got to go, Mom. I love you," I say to prevent myself from placing yet another wedge between my mother and me.

"Where are you anyway?"

"New York," I say and click my phone shut before I can hear her full exclamation of shock and dismay. Mom doesn't think I can handle New York. I've screwed up a few things in the past. She doesn't have a lot of faith in me.

As I slide my phone back into the pocket of Judy's coat, my fingers graze against something. I pull out an elegant golden cigarette case. I snap it open and take out a slim menthol cigarette. As I pause to light it, I catch a glimpse of myself in a window. I look like a woman who knows what she wants and who's sure of where she's going. I breathe in the smoke and let the essence of Judy swirl around in me. I flick my ashes on the sidewalk. Judy's ruby red lipstick stains the filter of my cigarette. I like that.

Author's Note: Kate Jonez

Most of my writing is filled with people who see themselves as deficient in some way. Their goal is to move to some wonderful new land or transform themselves into some more perfect being. Change is good. It keeps things interesting. Change is also hard. Really, really hard.

Aspiring is a game of cosmic whack-a-mole. There will always be some toothless cousin who'll spoil your bid to move up in the world, some instinct or illness or thought pattern that will foil your plans or some deeply held belief that will spring forth unexpectedly and mark you as being from another class, place or time. No one person can ever hold enough hammers to get every mole. Something is going to go wrong.

My obsession is with exploring how, no matter how earnest or heartfelt the desire, change, at least in the way imagined, is doomed to fail. Human nature is immutable. Individuals are everything they will ever be on the day they are born.

That sounds a bit bleak, but it's actually not. Tales of ugly ducklings turning into swans and poor boys making their fortunes don't resonate with me. Who wants to read about perfection? The more interesting story, the more truthful story, unfolds when people are tripped up by their own nature and something other than 'happily ever after' is the final outcome.

THE POINT

Johnny Worthen

Brian switches the LED light to the middle setting. He extends the telescoping lens out, turning the flashlight into a lantern and then places it in the center of his little table. He looks again at the two dead LEDs and shakes his head. They were supposed to last for decades. Cheap Chinese crap.

He lays out the plates, four settings of rugged cutlery and plastic plates. Four is all the table will hold but he has little doubt he'll have more guests than that.

"Sorry about pasta again," he says. "I have to finish that can of ground beef and we don't have any tortillas for tacos." He laughs. "Plus, we got plenty of water. Must be raining."

The little gas camp stove jabs spears of blue flame at the bottom of the aluminum pot. Brian shines his headlamp into the pot. He drops in a pinch of salt and covers it.

"Nearly boiling," he says.

He measures out Fusilli noodles and drops them on a scale. He removes five pieces, checks the weight, and records the number in a notebook.

"Gotta save room for dessert, right?"

He takes the lid from another pot and stirs the sauce; tomato paste, water and canned meat with one teaspoon of "Italian spice." The MRE meal is better but he's saving those.

He goes all out tonight. He feels good. He mixes a liter

of fruit punch and puts it on the table to breathe.

The boiling lid rattles and he drops the pasta into the water.

"Nearly done," he says.

He stirs the pot trying to keep focused on the task. Always on the task. The here and now. Only the now.

"Where was that kind of thinking before?"

"Dawn," he says to his wife. "You're early."

"The door was open," she says.

"Well," he says into the pot. "It'll only be a minute."

He shines his headlight into the saucepan and smells the meat again to reassure himself that it hasn't gone bad. The light on his forehead and the LED lamp on the table are the only lights in the bunker. He shines his light down the hallway to the storage rooms and chemical toilet and thinks to switch on a light down there. Then he remembers his batteries are growing weak and he doesn't feel like peddling for an hour to charge them tonight. He has enough light. His guests don't need any.

On the other side of the dining room, down the hallway, he sees the inner door ajar. A knot of clothesline stretches from its apex across the airlock to the green blast door beyond. Worn socks and underwear hang from the line like gray leaves or Dali's clocks. His headlight catches the silver chips in the far door where he'd first found the new welds and beat at them with all he had.

He turns back to the pasta.

"Zozar's here," says Dawn.

"I know."

"Of course I'm here. Where else would I be?"

"Scaring little boys in hell perhaps," says Dawn.

"The mouth on you," Lady Zozar says.

"And Michel," Dawn says. "Of course, Michel. And Saul and Three-Rabbit."

"Calm down Dawn," says Brian. "You're always so reactionary."

"Ha!" she says.

He turns off the stove and plucks pasta out with a fork and arranges it on his plate. He dumps the sauce on top of it. It's more than he wants, but he has to finish the meat today. He'll eat less tomorrow.

He takes his food to the table and sits down. He pours himself a glass of punch and turns off his headlight. He sighs in satisfaction; a task done, a moment of triumph. Then a sudden panic. Next task. What now? Do something now.

"Time for dinner," he sings cheerfully. He looks at the vacant chairs around his table, the empty plates and dry glasses, and hears nothing. He closes his eyes and listens hard.

There'd been a mouse for a while, back in the storage rooms. He'd listened to it at night and wondered how he'd gotten in. He never saw it, but at times he heard it. He hasn't heard it for months now. He wonders if it left or died. No matter; it's gone now and the bunker is quiet, silent as a grave. Like usual.

"Where were we?" he says.

"I told you the end was coming," says Lady Zozar.

"You frightened a child," says Brian's mother. "You should be ashamed of yourself."

"Mom," says Brian. "Your manners."

"Look— the mother blames a woman her son met once at a carnival," says Lady Zozar. "I don't think I'm worried."

The carnival was a throwback, a sideshow of the county fair which itself was a throwback to an agrarian lifestyle no longer lived in Brian's time. His mother had taken him there with Stan, her new boyfriend, for a cheap date with cheaper beer. She'd given Brian money and sent him off.

Alone, he'd seen the animals, the stalls of horses and goats, pigs and geese, until he could name them all by smell. He'd wandered the halls of quilts and amateur oil paintings, woodcarvings and coin collections and then gone out onto the midway.

Dust, kicked up from the animal pens, hung like thin

fog over the park. The late afternoon sunshine illuminated it into a pervasive tangerine glow making Brian feel like he was walking through a 30-watt light bulb. He bought an elephant ear, greasy and hot out of the fryer and followed it up with a snow cone and cotton candy before dropping three dollars on the dime skip. He wanted the signed basketball, but of course he didn't win a thing.

He bought tickets for the rides. He swung in the Tilt-A-Whirl until his elephant ear complained. He rode the Ferris wheel and scanned the fair looking for his mother and Stan coming out of the exhibit halls but didn't see them. At dark he'd have to be at the flagpole to meet them. Stan would be drunk by then, he was sure, and his mother would be angry. It was an established routine.

At dusk, the light turned ochre and he headed back. The heat and the color made him think of fires, but he smelled only dust and fry grease. Then he saw the tent.

"Lady Zozar— Prophesies and Fortunes."

He had tickets enough, and he went in.

The tent was straight out of an Agatha Christie novel; Victorian table and rugs, frills on the lampshades, embroidered chairs. It was kitsch, but at the time, Brian, only twelve years old, had never seen the like before. The exotic shapes and vibrant colors glowing in the odd sunlight aptly set the stage for an otherworldly encounter.

"Would you like to know the future?" she asked.

He jumped. He hadn't seen her on the settee clothed in veils.

"Yes," he whispered.

"Do you have your tickets?"

He handed her all he had.

"This is a lot."

"Tell it all to me," he said.

"Okay," she said. "Sit down."

With a flourish, she placed a crystal ball in the center of the table and winked at him.

"I don't need the ball," she said. "But people expect it."

"How do you see the future?"

"I look inside and where it folds, it comes out ahead."

He nodded like he understood and reminded himself to blink.

"Give me your hands," she ordered.

She clasped them across the table top on either side of the ball. Lady Zozar took a deep breath and rolled her eyes back into her head.

An electric shock ran up Brian's arms and spasmed his muscles.

Lady Zozar held tight.

"Are you sure you want to know," she rasped. "The future is a choice, but I have seen far."

Brian swallowed. "Yes," he said. "What do you see?"

"It will take your life," she said in a voice barely recognizable as feminine. It was like a demon spoke out of her mouth.

"What is it?"

"The prophecy!"

The room seemed colder suddenly and the sweat on his back chilled him. He shuddered. "The end of the world is nigh!"

"That was it?" says Michel. "What kind of cliché is that?"

"You're one to talk," says Dawn.

"Scared him to death," says Brian's mother.

"What?" says Lady Zozar. "I did good that time. I was right."

"Were you?" says Brian taking a bite of pasta.

"He still doesn't see it," says Dawn. "Idiot."

"Don't talk about my son that way," says Brian's mother. "He's a good boy."

"The battery under the table was a cheap trick," Dawn says to Zozar.

"It got the customer's attention."

Brian rolls his shoulders to work out an imagined cramp. He shakes salt onto his dinner and eats some.

He had been scared but also excited. He knew a secret.

And it was not just any secret— it was *the* secret.

He'd started his research that night. The first thing he'd done when he got home was look up the word 'nigh.'

"You wouldn't go to school," says his mother. "I didn't know why."

"I went," he says. "After a while."

"After you were a month behind your classmates," she says. "You almost failed the sixth grade."

"Are you piling on me too, Mom?" Brian says into his pasta.

"It's why she's here," says Dawn. "It's why we're all here; to hash this out."

"You're here for the company," he says.

"If you say so," says Dawn.

"He got through high school," says his mother. "Top twenty percent of his class. He got into three colleges."

"Because you made him," says Dawn.

"That's what mothers do."

"I think she means that he'd have done nothing if you hadn't made him," says Michel.

"What was the point?" says Brian.

Dawn laughs.

Brian cringes at her cackling. He doesn't remember it being so shrill.

"He learned French," says his mother. "He's a good boy."

"He learned French so he could read Nostradamus," says Dawn. "He told me so."

"And I am flattered," says Michel.

Brian wishes he could see him. It is too dark where he is and he's not that far gone. No. Not that far.

He knows Michel's face though; the keen eyes and scholarly beard printed in the front pages of all the books. Michel de Nostredame. Nostradamus. Brian knows his face better than his own wife's. But of course Dawn's face changed over time— it grew older and angrier whereas Michel's was always as solid as a wood carving, implacable and wise.

Dawn is right. He learned French for the sole reason of reading Nostradamus' prophesies in their original text. He needed also a grounding in Italian, Latin and Greek to make any sense of them, but that was all right. It gave him something to do in college while he waited for the end.

"Those were your best years," Dawn says.

"Why do you say that?"

"You had friends then."

"Not really," he says.

He hadn't known people. He joined study groups and sat by the same people, but he didn't think of them as friends. They were people he knew, like he knew the room numbers and street names. No reason to get close to anyone. What was the point? He was living in the last minutes of the planet and he knew it.

"And you were terrible company," says Dawn. "You told me."

He had tried to talk to people a couple of times. He was attracted to Beverly and told her his secret. She'd laughed at first and called him silly.

"What else should I have done?" says Beverly.

"You dumped me," he says.

"You were creepy," she says. "And such a downer."

"But you slept with me."

"You're welcome," she says.

He'd not told anyone else at college his secret. He kept his opinions and knowledge to himself. It wasn't hard. College students like the sound of their own voices and he could sit quietly and let them talk. He didn't contribute or agree or disagree. What was the point? They'd all be dead soon. They misinterpreted him, of course. He was called a good listener and counted among their friends, but he wasn't. For years after, they'd sent him Christmas cards and wedding invitations, birth announcements and stray emails. But he never answered them and after a while they stopped.

"I don't know about those being my best years," Brian

says. "We had some, didn't we, Dawn? We had a few."

"You should have graduated," says his mother before Dawn can answer.

When the money his father left no longer covered his tuition, he dropped out. He'd gotten five years of college out of the fund, but no degree. He never rounded out his electives. He had a disaster of a transcript; ancient languages and history, religious studies and astronomy, but nothing to earn him a degree let alone a job. Had he focused on any one aspect, taken the higher level classes, after five years he might have been able to find a job at a college somewhere. Maybe. But he hadn't. All he'd done was look for clues that would prove the prophecy right. The end of the world was nigh.

"I got a job," he says.

"It was a good job," says Tom Jeffrey, his boss from Crazy J's. "You made good money didn't you?"

"It wasn't terrible," says Brian.

"He could sell a car to anyone," jokes Tom in his boisterous way that carried across the lot. "I used to say he could sell ice to an Eskimo."

"I wasn't that good."

"Sure you were," says Tom. "You made good money. What'd you make from me?"

"Forty."

"Forty thousand dollars in commission for what? Half a year?"

"Seven months."

"You were going places."

"He's just a friendly person," says his mother. "Everyone loves him."

"He lied," says Dawn. "He lied to everyone."

"He did not."

"He did. That's how he sold so many cars. He lied because he couldn't see a reason not to."

"What did it matter?" says Brian.

"Brian's mantra!" says Dawn and cackles again.

"He was a natural."

"He was a charlatan," says Michel.

Dawn laughs louder. "You all are!" she yells.

"Forty-thousand bucks and you blew it in a month," says Tom.

"A couple months," says Brian. "Traveling Europe, bribing people to read books."

"See, he was getting out in the world, having adventures."

Dawn won't stop laughing.

Brian chews his pasta like he's mad at it.

"I saw Europe," he mutters.

"The inside of moldy reading rooms and rained out train stations," says Dawn.

"You weren't there," he says.

"Did I have to be?"

"What did you find?" asks Three Rabbit. He doesn't talk much so when he does Brian pays attention. He likes to imagine him in long colorful feathers and armor. He can't help but imagine him in profile with a strong Mesoamerican nose and jaguar cape.

"I found prophesies that had come true."

"Coincidence," says Dawn.

"Won't you shut up!" Brian turns around expecting to face her, but there is only the empty hallway. His shadow casts a dark silhouette against the peeling green blast door in the distance.

He stretches his neck and takes a breath before turning back.

"Henry the Second," he mutters.

"What is that?" says Lady Zozar.

Michel quotes his translated quatrain: "The young lion will overcome the older one, On the field of combat in a single battle; He will pierce his eyes through a golden cage, Two wounds made one, then he dies a cruel death."

"King Henry the Second of France was killed by the Comte de Montgomery in 1559. They both had lions on their shields. The lance went through Henry's visor."

"The visor was the cage?" asks Zozar.

"Yes," says Michel. "One shard of the lance hit him in the eye, another the temple."

"And the whole world shook," says Dawn. "Who the hell were the people anyway? This is what the future wants us to know? That two noble twats had a jousting accident? Dime a dozen prophecy."

"What about the atomic bomb," says Brian.

Nostradamus repeats the quatrain from Brian's memory. "Near the gates and within two cities, There will be scourges the like of which was never seen, Famine within plague, people put out by steel, Crying to the great immortal God for relief."

"How does that translate to an atomic bomb?" asks Lady Zozar.

"You're in the business," says Dawn. "You should know."

"Could mean anything," says Tom. "It sounds bad though. I'll give him that."

"It's shit," says Dawn.

"It's not shit," says Brian. "Michel. You tell them."

"What can I say?"

"Didn't your prophecies go until like 3900 AD?" asks Dawn. "So no end of the world in the foreseeable future? Get it? Foreseeable future." That cackle again.

Brian drags his fork over his plate. "That's open to interpretation," he says.

"But Zozar's trick convinced you?"

"The *Bible* is clear," says Saul. "The End Times are upon us."

Cackling.

Brian had left Europe with the last of his money and sailed to Israel. It was easier to travel then, before 9/11 and the Gulf Wars.

He hadn't gone to the Wailing Wall, the Mount of Olives, or the Dome on the Rock. He hadn't gone to Bethlehem, Gethsemane or Masada. He'd gone straight to Armageddon.

He'd learned it is a real place, a valley between Nazareth and the West Bank. There's a modern kibbutz there called Megiddo and there's a hill overlooking the valley and the kibbutz called Tel Megiddo, or Mount Megiddo in English. Armageddon means literally "Mountain of Megiddo." It is there that Brian made his pilgrimage.

"That's living!" teases Dawn.

"That's how you blew your money?" says Tom.

Brian nods.

He'd stayed there a month. Every day he'd wake up in the hostel, remember where he was, and shiver in fright and anticipation. As fast as he could he'd race up the mountain and find a place to watch the plain as if he were the first person let into a concert. He'd sit there all day looking at the dry desolate valley, watching dust devils skip across the rocks and fade away, expecting at any moment the earth to crack open and the world to be destroyed.

At dusk, when it was too dark to see, he'd head back to the town and eat. He'd fill his water bottles and go to bed, ready to do it all again the next day.

The people didn't ask him what he was doing. No one talked to him after the first day. They watched him with a distant nervousness that reinforced his knowledge that he had a secret.

After a month, sunburned and dirty, he boarded a bus and left. He'd seen nothing, but he'd sensed the truth. He was sure the end was near. It was in the sharp stones that had shredded his shoes and in the dust that colored the air and reddened his eyes. It was in his mind full of French verse and Biblical quotes. It was in the words of the prophets carrying signs in Tel-Aviv, the graffiti on the walls of JFK. The end was nigh. He knew it.

Back home he waited in his room for it to happen.

He spent days and nights furiously studying the *Book of Revelations*, imagining an author, Saul, bent over the pages with a pen, inflamed with the voice of God, seeing the end times and interpreting the visions the best he could.

"It was all I could do," says Saul.

"You didn't write it," says Dawn. "No single person wrote it."

"So I'm an amalgam," he says. "It's easier to conceive that way. We do the best we can."

When the world didn't end right away, Brian waited longer. When he ran out of money, he sold his things and waited again.

When he was kicked out of his apartment, he got a job packing candles and got into a smaller apartment.

"I was so worried about you," his mother says. "You were twenty-eight years-old and wasting away."

"How long did you sit in that room waiting for the end?" asks Tom.

"Five years," he says. "I studied the prophecies."

"Which didn't come true," says Dawn.

"I had to do something, sweetie," says his mother. "I hope you know that."

"It's fine," he says.

She'd committed him. At least that's how he saw it. It was called 'voluntary in-patient treatment,' but his mother made him stay, so what was the difference?

"You were skin and bones," she says. "You hadn't cleaned your house in a year. The bathroom— oh, god the bathroom."

"I'm eating here, Mom."

"Sorry, Honey."

The room they'd given him was eight feet by twelve feet and he shared it with no one. He had a view of the lawn over trimmed, green hedges and could see the freeway in the distance as a black ribbon during the day and a river of lights at night.

He had new clothes from his mother, clean sheets and a bed. His mother didn't visit him.

"I was heartbroken," she said.

"You were with Andy then right?" says Dawn. "In Tahoe?"

"It was too far to drive," she says defensively. "And, like I said, I couldn't bear to see him like that."

"It's fine, Mom," he says.

"You were in 3G," says Dawn. "I was in 2A. Different wing and seven rooms away."

"You were insane," Brian says.

Dawn laughs, a full-throated, tear-pulling laugh that makes Brian smile. "I have issues," she says.

"So did I," says Brian.

"Did?"

He couldn't see any reason to keep his secret from his doctor. He'd told him the first session. He put it all out there, his visit to Lady Zozar, his studies, trips and knowledge, all the dominoes up to the clinic. The doctor had listened and nodded and taken notes. He let him talk until he stopped. He hadn't challenged his interpretation of Nostradamus, the *Book of Revelation* or the apocryphal Delphic Oracles. He'd listened with an interested and non-judgmental expression for two straight hours.

"You were good at that," says Brian.

"It was my job," says his doctor. "You were interesting."

"But crazy."

"Not the clinical description I'd use," he says. "I prefer 'obsessive.'"

He wasn't required to talk in group sessions and didn't. While his doctor worked with him in private, he listened to the others' problems and tried to care. It all seemed so stupid to be worried about drugs or sex-addiction. He found himself glancing at his watch not because he was bored necessarily, though he often was, but so he could know the exact minute it would all end. Somehow he got it into his mind that it would all happen at quarter past something. Every hour, at fifteen minutes past, he'd tense up for a few seconds.

"You didn't tell me about that," says the doctor.

"What was the point?"

"You were cute," says Dawn. "You were a good listener."

Brian shrugs. His meal is half done and all cold. He rearranges noodles into sauce camps on opposite sides of his plate.

"You knew I was there for control issues," she says. "You should have seen this coming."

"You lack a sense of scale and proportion," says the doctor.

"Road rage. Simple thing. Totaled two cars and the bitch deserved it."

"Which time?" asks Tom.

Dawn laughs. "Touché."

When Brian had finally talked in group, he'd made enough progress in private sessions to admit that he might have been mistaken about his secret.

"It's taken all my time," he'd said. "All my energy. All my thought. Everything. I'm waiting for the shoe to drop."

He'd said it in a way that made it seem like he was sorry, but he was just telling the truth.

"Everyone's going to die," Dawn says.

"You can't live your whole life afraid," the doctor had told him.

But he was wrong.

"Mostly wrong," says Dawn. "We had a few good years."

"I'm glad you think so."

He and Dawn got out the same day and were married the same month. They moved into a little house in the suburbs and made plans to start a family.

Brian found translation work with a law firm with pan-Atlantic clients and Dawn waited tables. Mother died two years later and left him enough money to build the shelter.

"That money was for my grandchildren," she says. "I told you I wanted you to save the money for my grandchildren."

"He didn't see the point," says Dawn. "Tick tock, tick tock. The end of the world is nigh."

"You did this," mother says to Zozar.

"Where were you?" she counters.

"Reno and Tahoe," says Brian. "The bars at night."

"Don't blame me," she says. "I did my best. You're a grown man."

"I tried to stop him," says Dawn. "I saw it creeping in. You hooked him again Three Rabbit."

"Western man is so stupid," says the chief. "You do not understand circles."

"We're the pinnacle of culture," says Michel. "We've conquered science."

"And have the Holy writ," adds Saul.

"You named the end of the world," says Brian. "Your calendar proclaimed it."

"You fool," says Three Rabbit. "Does your world end on December 31st? No. It ends a year to begin another. That is how calendars work."

"But your calendar spanned centuries."

"It was a long calendar, but a cycle nonetheless. You fearful, foolish people."

"You blew it all on this thing," says Dawn. "You paid premium prices to get it installed before the big day and you blew everything we had. No, you blew more than we had. You took out a second mortgage and borrowed. You ruined us."

"You didn't seem so upset that night," he says. "You looked grateful."

"You scared me then too," she says. "Yeah, I sat in here with you for a couple of days while nothing— absolutely nothing happened outside. Then I left."

"The prophecy," he mumbles.

"Which one?" asks Three Rabbit. "I never made one."

"Michel. Yours," he says.

"Brian, I was poor. I wrote almanacs. I needed the money. Why do you think I wrote in code and verse and riddles?"

"To keep the church off you."

"If I had the real word of God do you think I'd worry about that?"

"God told you to obfuscate," says Saul. "So that only the

wise would understand."

"And only the fools would believe," he says. "Michel, it was just riddles and games meant to sell books."

"Doesn't matter why or how as long as it's true," Brian mutters, tears forming in his eyes. "It is still true regardless of the source."

"Hopeless," says Dawn. "See?"

"Saul," says Brian. "You tell them. The horsemen, the wars, plagues. The second coming."

"I'd like to Brian, but you know it's not that way. It's politics. It's all about scaring people to make people submit. Scare them out of their money. Keep them in line."

"But they all say the same thing," he says. "All the prophets see the end of the world."

"'Live every day as if it's your last,'" says Dawn, "'And one day you'll be right.'"

Brian's crying now.

"But you didn't, did you, Hon?" she says. "Even with me you didn't. You snuggled with me, but you always had one eye on the window looking for the asteroid. One foot in the grave ready to jump in."

"Please no," he says.

"You never wanted this bunker to survive," she says. "You wanted to live long enough— just long enough to say 'I knew it.'"

"I wanted to live."

"When? After everyone was dead? Bullshit, Brian. If you wanted to live, you'd have lived. You had your chance. This is what you wanted. This is your prophecy come true. You're welcome."

"You didn't need to do this," he says.

"Maybe not," she says. "But it's what you wanted."

His sobs echo off the concrete walls and bounce back in mocking stereo. He can't focus on his meal for the tears in his eyes.

"It might have happened," he says. "It could be happening right now."

"Tell yourself it did," she says. "But we know the prophecies were bullshit."

"Mine wasn't," says Lady Zozar.

"True, but he doesn't understand it."

"The end of the world is nigh!" he screams into the darkness. "What's there to understand?"

"What did she say?" asks Three Rabbit.

"She said 'the end of the world is nigh.'"

"Before that."

Brian wipes his eyes. "Um, she said, 'There was a choice and it will take your life.'"

"What was 'it'?"

"The prophecy," says Brian. "She said, 'The prophecy will take your life.'"

"Bingo!" calls Dawn. "We have a winner."

"My life."

"Gone. Wasted and unused. No loss."

He throws his plate across the table, flipping the light onto the floor. Another LED blinks out.

"How much food do you have left?"

"More than half," he says.

"So another three years?"

"About that," he says.

"And the water's holding up?"

"No radio though. You must have cut that."

"Must have."

"Am I going to die in here?"

The words echo off the empty room and back into his ears.

"You didn't need to bury me in here."

"It was a bit of an overreaction," says his mother.

"We all have issues," Dawn says. "It's not as if I didn't warn him."

"Someone will come looking for me."

"Who? You know no one. You did nothing. You don't even have memories to keep you alive."

"I have memories."

"Of waiting to die," she says. "Of hoping to die. Of expecting to die. That's what you got. That's it. You have that. You're right where you should be. Dead."

"I'm not dead!" Again he screams, but only he hears it.

He takes a deep breath and focuses on the routine. He has to clean up the plate. It's not broken. He broke the last one and the one before that, but this plastic one is more durable.

He wipes off the floor and carries his dishes to the sink. He hums to keep the voices silent and makes his mind focus on the narrow beam of his headlight as he cleans up his meal.

He finds his way back to his bunk, but it is only eight o'clock. That's a guess. The clock battery died last year and he had to guess the time to reset it. No matter. In his world it's eight and he doesn't go to bed until ten.

He pulls out his tattered book of prophecies and reads a while. He speaks the words out loud to hear his voice and to keep the others silent.

If he lets it get too quiet, they might talk to him again. At least he's not seeing them. Not yet. Three years and he's only hearing them.

At ten he climbs into his bed and turns off the light.

"Am I going to die in here?" he mutters half asleep.

"No honey," answers Dawn. "You died years ago."

Author's Note: Johnny Worthen

Two of my obsessions appear in "The Point" and though I can remember precisely the moment the first infected me, the second, the underlying one, the one that is always there in everything I write, I cannot explain.

It was a rare mother-son date, a dinner and a movie. I don't remember the movie, but I can see that booth now. It had red leather upholstery and the flickering candle in a red faceted jar. I was ten years old. We had garlic bread and my mother told me about Nostradamus. She scared the living hell out of me. She meant well. It was in the late '70s and Nostradamus was again in vogue. An interesting topic. My mother had a book. She told me about the prophecies with the zeal of a believer and then talked about the sun turning to blood and Armageddon. It was all very matter of fact. It was all too much for me to hear.

I spent years worrying about it. I lost sleep over it. I talked to everyone I could about it. The only thing that eased my mind happened back in the '80s when a friend told me about the Mayan Calendar predicting the end in 2012. That gave me thirty years. I latched onto those and carried on but always with a worry and watching, looking for comets, following the Doomsday Clock, tracking flus and civil wars. I'm still not over it. 2012 has come and gone but I feel the end closer than ever.

There is always a scent of doom in my writing, and often a stench of it. Time is always short. But there is more.

This doom, I believe, may have metastasized into the other obsession I find buried in every single work I've ever penned. It may be a product of that Italian restaurant, I don't know, but there is death in everything I write.

I don't always mean to have it there, but I always find it when I look back. In my comedies there is death. I once wrote a children's Christmas poem about kittens and the body count was three. It is always in my writing because it is always in my mind. If it's not clearly on the page, I find death waiting in the margins, implied and menacing. It's always there waiting for its certain and tragic moment, inexorable and preordained, like the end of the world.

CALLIGRAPHY

James Everington

The lettering was a light brown colour against Blake's skin, which was pale from being indoors so much. Each individual letter was small but elegantly formed: handwritten was the word that came to mind. And with some care. He traced the loops and spirals of the words across his face. They never once crossed. He couldn't feel anything beneath his fingertips other than skin and stubble.

He was at a loss how to react. He had risen this morning to find his face in the mirror covered in elegant, cursive writing. Although he was sure it was in English, Blake couldn't tell what any of the words said.

Who was responsible? The writing looked so precise and deliberate there could be no doubt human agency was behind them. But Blake had no family, few friends— and those acquaintances he did have were as staid and clumsy as Blake himself. None of them were practical jokers or would have had the ingenuity for a prank such as this even if they were. And besides, Blake hadn't seen any of them for weeks, months, now that he thought of it.

So what explanation could there be?

He scrubbed at his face with soap and then with a pumice stone, but the writing didn't come off or fade; if anything it looked even more prominent against the skin he'd scrapped raw.

If he could just read what it said, that would surely explain things.

But the more he looked the more unintelligible the words on his face seemed.

It's because you're seeing them back to front in the mirror, Blake thought. You need someone else to read them for you. He felt nervous at the idea. Blake had long ago decided to live a life of seclusion. The avaricious nature of people in both their dealings with him and the wider world had always left him at a loss. He had no wish to be part of the world's schemes and sins and his inheritance, used modestly, meant he didn't have to be.

The faint sound of a peal of bells came from outside and echoed around the bathroom. He couldn't recall ever having heard the local church from his house, but Blake wasn't a religious man and he assumed he had just never noticed before.

Realising he would have to go outside he dressed, clumsily knotting his tie without looking in the mirror. He checked his keys and handkerchief were in his pocket, a ritual reassurance before stepping into the chaotic world outside. He fumbled at his jacket buttons, as if they were the wrong way round.

When he opened his front door, his first thought was that the day was very bright, and his second that the bells, which were still ringing, were very clear. It was a Sunday then. He hadn't thought it so, but Blake often lost track of his days.

As he took a hesitant step up the street, a front door opened. An old lady stepped out, dressed in her Sunday best: a fake fur coat and ponderous hat. She didn't appear to have noticed Blake and he didn't think he'd be able to call out to her because his throat was so tight, but he managed it.

"Excuse... excuse me?"

Her smile seemed kind as she turned to him. He wondered if she couldn't see the writing on his face or if she was just too polite to let on she could. "Hello dear," she said, and Blake relaxed somewhat. She was only an old lady, after all.

"I need your help," he began. "My face..." He didn't know how to explain his predicament. "My face," he said again, helplessly. Nevertheless the old lady nodded as he spoke, as if he were telling her things she already knew. She took his hand almost eagerly and he was surprised at the warmth in her old skin.

Her eyes were bright.

"I found you first," she said, as if finishing aloud a thought in her head.

Although Blake didn't know what she meant by that, he felt an odd feeling of pride, of having something to crow about to others. He didn't know where the feeling came from. His face felt flushed, from the shame of showing her its words, he supposed.

"What does it say?" he said.

"You need to come to the church," the old woman said, "with me. There's answers there."

He didn't know whether she was talking about the handwriting or something more general.

Still holding his hand, she led him to the top of the street and then surprised him by turning in the opposite direction from the local parish church. But it was the direction from which the sound of bells was coming.

The main road was deserted, as if it were still dawn. There was no traffic, none of the ill-tempered pedestrians and cyclists that Blake remembered. The gaudy advertising hoardings had been taken down, and there was no dog shit or litter to avoid on the ground. What exactly have I been scared of out here? Blake thought. It even smelt fresh.

As he walked with the old lady another door opened and two young girls in identical pink dresses ran out. They stopped when they saw Blake, and stared at his face. He looked down, not wanting them to see.

The parents came out after the girls, smiling indulgently at them and hurrying them towards the pavement.

"Ha!" the old woman said under her breath, with a spite

that unnerved Blake for it seemed so out of place as the family, who were all smiles, started walking alongside them.

The two girls were staring at Blake, too shy to speak to him. He wasn't used to children but gave them a small wave.

"Hello," one of the girls said but then the other pinched her, and she cried out. The parents ignored her and carried on smiling. Blake looked away and felt somehow responsible. Even such a small thing reminded him of all the reasons why he had avoided other people.

More people joined their group, coming out from unremarkable looking houses on either side of the road. They walked towards the sound of the bells. Soon the crowd was twenty or thirty people strong, walking on both the pavement and the road. Blake felt an unusual thrill at being with so many other people, at the sense of shared purpose. Until he caught someone looking at him oddly, and he remembered the words he bore on his face.

You are still different and alone.

The old lady pulled at his hand as her pace quickened. She was looking away from him and directly ahead; Blake looked too.

He couldn't believe he'd lived all his life in this neighbourhood and not seen the church before. It was true he didn't venture outside much— but never to have noticed this? Its spire was at least as tall again as that of the parish church, and so smooth it didn't seem to be made of individual bricks but all of a piece. The stone was a light pink hue, the colour of a soft sunset. The stained glass windows blazed with an interior light. They depicted sins and saints and creatures that Blake didn't recognise.

The crowd of people (now surely close to a hundred) didn't pause as they reached the church. As a result they were all pressed tightly against each other as they passed through the wooden doors. Blake was unable to breathe, his old panic tight in his chest. It was like the one time he'd dared catch the tube— he'd had to get off a single stop later, unable to bear the press of bodies against his. But this time the feeling only lasted a second or two and then he was inside the church.

It was almost as light inside as without, for the interior of the church was suffused with pink light from the windows and seemed warm and inviting. It flickered as if with candlelight without there being any obvious candles present. From above came the faint, chiming echo of the bells.

The old lady had let go of his hand in the crush. He was at a loss what to do next, when he saw a young woman gesturing that the seat next to her was free. Despite her age there was something old-fashioned about her look: a demure summer dress and pale, faultless skin. On the other side of her sat a young man with almost the same features.

Blake sat down and was surprised when the woman immediately put her hand on his leg and smiled at him. He tried to smile back but he was so self-conscious about the writing on his face (and of her hand) that he daren't meet her gaze. Blake wasn't much used to female company. The young man on the other side of her had ceased to look friendly and was rigidly ignoring them both.

"Sorry about... this," Blake said to the woman, making a clumsy gesture towards his face.

She smiled, flushed prettily.

"Oh," she said, "that makes you interesting..."

"For god's sake..." the man on the other side of her muttered.

Maybe they aren't sister and brother, Blake thought.

"Interesting?" he said.

"Exciting..."

His desperation to know why he had been marked out overcame his normal fear of strangers. "Look," he said, leaning towards the woman, "Can you tell me what it says?"

"Oh yes," the woman said, and she kissed him full on the mouth, her tongue parting his lips. Both her hands were on the side of his face and Blake shivered as he imagined her fingers moving over what was written there. His own hands twitched in his lap; he was about to raise them (whether to touch her or push her away he didn't know) when she sat back and smiled to herself, not looking at him.

Blake looked round guiltily (although it hadn't been his fault) but the rest of the congregation were staring straight ahead towards the lectern. The woman was also looking ahead as if the kiss had never happened and he was too confused to risk speaking to her again. What sort of church is this? Blake thought.

The bells stopped ringing, and a priest stepped to the lectern. At least Blake assumed the man was a priest, although he wore salmon-pink robes rather than black, and had no collar.

The congregation rose and Blake stood with them. They sang a hymn that he didn't recognise in such pure, sweet voices that it brought tears to his eyes. Next week, he thought, I'll learn the words for next week.

The congregation sat; Blake leant forward along with everyone as the priest started to speak.

"Today is a special day," the priest said, "in our calendar. A day of signs, a day of forgiveness."

Blake listened to every word; he remembered the old lady's claim that there were answers here. "We renounce our sins and ask for them to be forgiven. But forgiveness can only come from without. Today is a special day in our calendar, a day of signs, and a day when we welcome an outsider into our church."

There was the sound of wood against stone as the congregation shifted in their pews to look at Blake. He couldn't meet their gaze.

"I found him," the old lady said in a loud whisper from behind him. He stood up and the woman sitting next to him trailed a finger across his thighs as he did so.

The priest gestured Blake forward; his look was not unkind. Blake walked down the central aisle. The soft, pink-hued air flickered. When he reached the front, the priest touched Blake's face and his fingers softly traced the lines of the calligraphy. So he can see it then, Blake thought. He can read it.

"Would you like to know," the priest said, "what it says?"

"Yes, oh yes," Blake said.

The priest sighed.

"Know then," he said, "that we do this out of love."

Love, Blake thought, why did I always think of that as a trite word?

The priest gently touched Blake on the shoulder and he realised the man wanted him to kneel. As he did so he closed his eyes although he hadn't been told to. It just felt like the right thing to do.

Next week, he thought, you won't be the outsider next week.

The priest's fingers touched his face again, more firmly this time, and traced the writing there.

"Your sins," the priest said, in a deeper, louder voice than he'd used previously, "are these: Cravenness. Materialism. Intellectual arrogance. Homosexuality. Atheism. Aloofness from man. Greed for all things..."

Blake cried; just a few tears. He doubted if they would be enough to wash anything away. But why was he crying at all? He might be arrogant and he might be an atheist, but he wasn't a homosexual (and didn't believe it wrong, anyway). And he certainly wasn't greedy or...

"...Adultery," the priest continued, his fingers still moving over Blake's face. "Rapaciousness, Sottishness..."

But these aren't..., Blake thought. He became aware that the congregation behind him were shifting in their seats and shuffling their feet.

These aren't my sins.

The priest's hands continued to move over Blake's face; he spoke each word as if he were casting it aside. But to Blake it felt like the opposite, as if the words were seeping into him, as if the sins of others were being absorbed by his own body.

He was openly sobbing by the end, his face puffy and enflamed. He felt sick and bloated with all he'd just heard, sins both petty and terrible. When he stood, his legs wobbled as though he was physically weighed down, his body shivered as if with infection.

The priest's hands were gentle again as he guided Blake down the aisle towards the church doors.

The woman who had been so flirtatious with him looked away in disgust. The kindly old lady sneered at him with a smug look in her eyes.

"Out of love," the priest said again. There was no other sound. Then he roughly pushed Blake against the church doors which opened to let him stumble outside.

It was grey outside, so much so that it seemed unreal to Blake. There was a muffled roaring as if his ears were blocked. Off balance from being pushed, he fell against someone. "Piss off!" the man shouted, and pushed Blake from him. He started to apologise but the man had already turned away.

Somehow, he was suddenly on a busy street, and he was being pulled along by the crowd of people; his ears popped and noise burst over him in a wave. He turned round but couldn't see the church; in its place was a burger bar from which he could smell meat; his stomach turned.

Litter flapped away from a bin that was too full nearby, and a woman barged into him with her pram then swore at him like it was his fault. He stepped aside for her and heard the screech of a car horn.

He raised his hands to his face, but he couldn't feel anything beneath his fingertips other than skin. He turned to look at his face in the reflection of the burger bar windows but they were too covered in grime and gaudy posters for him to get a clear view.

The church..., he thought, and it was as though for a second he could still hear the bells chiming, until he realised it was the sound of sirens rushing closer.

All around him people were shouting and shoving. No one paid him much attention.

He didn't know where he was or how to get home.

It was cold, and he did his jacket up without thinking, for the buttons were the correct way round again.

Author's Note: James Everington

It sounds nothing more than a truism, I imagine, to suggest that one of my compulsions as a writer is words. Aren't all writers obsessed by words (or at least, all decent writers)? By the feel of them and the joy of what they can do?

Well yes. But like many writers, I think I also have a fear of words. I mistrust them, sometimes, the way they are so fickle, the way they can turn like a knife in the hand and cut you by meaning something other than the writer intended. The way sometimes they don't seem to mean anything at all. And so sometimes I write not just with language but about language. You can see it clearly in a story I wrote called "A Writer's Words" (from the collection *The Other Room*) and you can see it in "Calligraphy" too.

Words are both private and public; they are the bridge between inside and outside. It's a bridge that can be crossed both ways. Calligraphy came about when I thought about combining two ideas: a story about a guiltless (?) man being cast out as a scapegoat, and the idea of someone being infected by words from without. By words not just of another person but another place entirely.

There's something slippery about words, something treacherous, and maybe those of us who are so obsessed with them should be a bit less trusting of their easy magic.

THIS MANY

S.P. Miskowski

The costume appeared in a dream. In October, the temperature was still mild enough to keep the bedroom windows open at night. Maybe Lorrie's imagination was piqued by the mild vinegar scent of the blue jacarandas, slowly drying in the Pacific breeze.

In her dream, Lorrie stepped onto a dirt path at the bottom of a ravine. She followed its twisted incline all the way to her house, where the wooden gate stood open. Ahead of her, the trunks of the sycamore trees were etched white and gray against the lawn, while high above, a tiny fairy-like creature floated in midair. The creature seemed to be lit from within, her pink and ruby gown glowing, her diaphanous wings quivering.

Lorrie felt the color rise in her cheeks. Warm light spread from her neck to her chest and arms. She felt that she, too, was glowing.

When she awoke, Lorrie reached for her journal and quickly sketched the outfit she had seen. It was perfect, exactly what she wanted for Frances. The tricky bit would be the ruched velvet across the bodice. But she knew she could match the pink and ruby satin, and build a sheer set of wings. She had conquered more ambitious projects, including the fully decorated playhouse that stood disused in a far corner of the yard, discarded after one summer of sleepovers and outdoor games.

The crafts store on Aliso Way would have everything

she needed. Lorrie could gather all of the supplies without leaving her neighborhood. She decided to make this a selling point during the unavoidable conversation with Kirk. He was a sweetheart. He just worried too much about the budget, which was natural for an accountant. And he didn't understand the difference between buying a good, readymade outfit and making the extra effort to create a one-of-a-kind memory for their daughter. Lorrie had given up trying to explain. More and more often she fell back on her mother's example.

"She served macaroni and cheese for dinner, Kirk. Twice a week."

"So she was tired." Kirk said. "Single moms have a tough time."

"Macaroni?"

"I'm a little surprised you didn't demand sushi." He grinned.

"Not the point."

"Honey," Kirk said, rubbing the back of his neck. "What is the point?"

"This won't cost as much as you think. It just takes time. I can get everything we need at Hobby Hut..."

"Okay, okay," he said, winding down, as he always did. "Do what you want."

Lorrie was glad to sidestep the question of when she might return to work. Their most heated debates were over this. During the years since her generous maternity leave had become semi-permanent, Kirk had been promoted twice. They could live on his salary, even if they couldn't save or invest much.

Halfheartedly she'd begun to check a couple of job sites, but she didn't plan to call any of her contacts until after the holidays. Frances was in kindergarten this year, and there would be a million special moments to share. Where would the girl turn without her mom?

Lorrie thought back on all the school pageants and bake sales and kickball games her mother never attended.

Sometimes she sent a proxy, usually a sullen twenty-something named Nancy who wore black T-shirts and sunglasses and had bad skin. Nancy was the daughter of another legal secretary and the sight of her could make Lorrie freeze. She had imagined when she was a child that this was how all daughters of professional women turned out, dark and silent and only tenuously connected to the people around them, applauding on cue but never giving a damn about anything. Nancy, with her greasy brown hair parted on the side and her lips curled in a sneer, was no substitute for a mom. Only a real mom would sew an original gown and plan a perfect party.

During the second fitting, with a sheath of ruby fabric draped across her slender shoulders and the frame for fairy wings poised above her head, Frances announced her intention to be a witch for her birthday. Lorrie clenched the batch of straight pins between her teeth. She removed them and drew a clean breath before she spoke.

"Frances, remember how we talked about your wonderful dress?"

"Uh..."

"Mommy's been sewing all weekend to make you a fairy princess in time for the party."

"I want a black hat and boots!"

Frances did a bouncy dance step in place. Lorrie looked at the wire and satin and velvet lying all around her on the living room carpet.

"Sweetie," she said. "I don't think a black hat will be pretty with a fairy princess gown."

"I want a black dress, like Annie's got."

They had run into Gloria Shepherd with her seven-year-old, Annie, at the mall. Frances blurted out an invitation before Lorrie could stop her. Annie was wearing a witch costume, which Gloria had personalized with a few Goth touches including mascara, lipstick, and a black choker decorated with miniature skulls.

One glance at Annie's tough-girl style and Frances

started complaining. She reminded Lorrie that she had been Sleeping Beauty the previous year, and Strawberry Shortcake the year before that.

Lorrie could have killed Gloria Shepherd. All the way home she wondered about Gloria's shaky marriage to a much younger day trader. She also wondered who made the rules in the Shepherd family.

"But don't you want to be the star of your own party?" Lorrie asked, trying not to whine.

It was the kind of question her mother would have asked, playing on Lorrie's need to be the center of attention. Except Lorrie's mother, Caroline, would never have sewn a garment for her daughter. Anything she could afford pre-made, Caroline bought.

Her mother's scant free time had been sacred, reserved for facials, television, and naps. Lorrie only realized the macaroni and cheese dinners were not gourmet and her JC Penney clothes were not cool when she started first grade.

"I want a black hat with a pointy top," said Frances.

"Sweetie," Lorrie said.

She found herself fumbling for an answer a six-year-old would buy. Not griping about how much time she'd already spent on the dress. Not pointing out how adorable a honey-blonde girl with a cherubic smile would look with wings pinned to her shoulders and a petite, ruby-studded crown on her head. The 'pretty factor' wouldn't work, thanks to Gloria Shepherd and her future-heroin-addict daughter.

"Frances, it's bad luck."

The girl gazed at her mother with an expression of high seriousness. Her silence was difficult to read but Lorrie decided to press on while she had the advantage.

"Wearing black on your birthday is a no-no. I'm sure Annie won't wear black on her birthday."

"But," the girl thought hard. "It's almost Halloween."

"Oh, well, on Halloween, sure. You can be a witch to go trick or treating. I'm talking about your party, on Saturday.

It's bad luck to wear black on your birthday."

"Oh."

Lorrie felt a blush begin to rise from her jaw to her cheeks. Nevertheless, she accepted the victory. Next year she could never get away with such a lie. But now, for at least one more set of birthday photos, her daughter would be dazzling.

On Saturday, the air was still, and the cul-de-sac lay silent. The few neighbors who obsessed over their lawns had given up for the time being, even the old man next door, an octogenarian who loved to complain about the mess made by the jacarandas.

As of 1:15, no one had shown up. Lorrie poured a box of orange punch into a ceramic bowl and carried it out the patio door to a table on the lawn. The sycamores provided a light canopy and Lorrie had decided not to string the cheap plastic skeletons and pumpkins along the fence. If she couldn't afford the beautiful lanterns she really wanted, the trees would have to suffice as decoration.

Inside, in the foyer, she fussed with the strings on a bunch of helium-filled balloons. For a second, she entertained the idea of curling the ends with scissors to make them more festive.

"Stop," she told herself. "Just stop it."

The balloons were printed with the faces of trolls, witches, werewolves, and vampires. Lorrie wondered if they were too intense for the younger children. It was the sort of concern Kirk would label 'a first world problem.'

"I saw *Nightmare on Elm Street* when I was five," he must have told her a dozen times. "Look at me. I'm fine. Kids need to be scared sometimes. It's healthy. How else can they learn to work through their fears?"

Kirk was also the champion of bike-riding in the park without a helmet and rollerblading without kneepads. Whenever she threw a kids' party Lorrie sent Kirk to play golf and gave him an okay to smoke cigars at the pro club, after.

At 1:25 Karen arrived wearing surgical scrubs. Her twins were dressed as Hansel and Gretel. Hansel was in one of his moods.

"We had a disagreement about whether a Padres cap would be 'just as good' as this adorable, authentic-looking Tyrolean hat—"

"Monkey hat," Hansel grumbled.

"I found it at Kohl's. In the men's department."

"Retarded," the boy said.

Karen blushed. She lowered her voice and leaned close to Hansel.

"What did I tell you, my friend?"

Hansel studied his left hand.

Lorrie gave Frances a slight push forward.

"Welcome to my party," Frances said automatically, without smiling.

"Oh, look, kids!" Karen fussed. "Isn't the birthday girl beautiful?"

Frances stood, glum and wide-eyed, while they admired her costume.

"How old are you today?" Karen asked.

"This many," said Frances, holding up five fingers.

Lorrie gave her a look, and she corrected herself by adding the index finger of her left hand. "I mean, this many."

"So sweet," Karen cooed. "And oh my god, this dress is unbelievable. Haute couture again! Frances, you're a lucky little girl."

As soon as his mother was distracted, Hansel side-stepped her and headed down the hall. He slowed long enough to navigate the cluster of balloons, punched one of the troll faces, and then wandered toward the sugary aroma of the kitchen.

Gretel was still fiddling with the beaded buttons on her peasant blouse. When Karen raised her eyebrows, Gretel went indoors. Frances followed. Karen waited until the girls were out of earshot.

"Sorry my kids are such clots."

"It's okay."

"No, honestly, if they weren't so stupid, I'd sell them both. No offers yet."

"They're fine," Lorrie said. "Eight is a tough age."

"Don't be kind," Karen joked. "I'm thinking of having a maternity test."

"Sets of twins, switched at birth? What are the odds?"

"I'm clinging to this, Lorrie, don't shoot it down."

Both women punched the monster-faced balloons on their way down the hall. From outside came the first shrieks of children chasing one another.

A few minutes later the deluge began, and for the next half hour the hostess was busy non-stop. She greeted everyone at the door with an apology for the imperfect weather. There were thin clouds over Endless Vista extending north and east beyond Sunswept Mesa and Glittering Sky. Not enough clouds to ruin the day, but there could be sprinkles of rain later.

"I ordered a much better afternoon," Lorrie joked more than once. With Frances in tow, she ushered all of the guests through her kitchen and on through the patio doors to the back lawn, where games and treats awaited.

"Why can't I just play?" Her daughter asked between arrivals.

"Sweetie, this is how it's done. The birthday girl greets her guests," Lorrie said, eliciting only a sigh and a shrug.

By the time Gloria rang the doorbell most of the other neighborhood parents had shown up, bearing gifts and dutifully dressed in medical scrubs as Lorrie had instructed. Most of them stood sipping punch under the sycamores while their children played tag across the lawn.

Gloria handed over a cake on a tray with a makeshift foil cover, and then scratched at her maroon hair. Before entering the house with Annie the Goth witch, she asked if it was all right to smoke.

"Just one. Outdoors, of course."

"Afraid not," said Lorrie with what she hoped was a

withering smile. "On top of everything else, we're coping with asthma. One of Karen's twins, Harris, that's Hansel. Or maybe it's Tina, that's Gretel. I've forgotten which. Anyway, sorry, no smoking."

"Annie had a touch of asthma when she was little, but we got her over that with swimming lessons."

Frances had crept up behind Lorrie to peek out at her idol on the doorstep. Annie shifted her weight but ignored the younger girl's adoring expression.

"Wow," said Gloria. "That's a hell of a dress, Frannie."

Lorrie winced. She couldn't abide nicknames.

"Is that a prom dress?" Annie asked, wrinkling her nose prettily under the wide brim of her black hat, and giving Frances an insouciant once-over.

Lorrie could have strangled her.

"Mom made it so I have to wear it," Frances replied, and rolled her eyes.

Annie laughed. Frances laughed. Gloria laughed. And it seemed to Lorrie that every minute she'd spent stitching and hemming, to say nothing of bandaging her needle-pricked fingers, had been dismissed as nothing. The way Kirk dismissed her bread-baking and crocheting or the mommy-daughter ballet class.

"I like your costume too, Annie," Lorrie said. "Are you Hermione, or just any old witch?"

Even Gloria looked surprised.

Lorrie flushed red. Insulting a seven-year-old, she thought, what kind of mom does that?

To cover her embarrassment, she ushered everyone out to the back yard. She took the lid off Gloria's cake. It was pathetic. She felt better almost at once.

In the kitchen, Lorrie placed the cake on the marble countertop in front of Karen and sighed. They tried looking at it from different angles. No use. It was Gloria's standard-issue coconut vanilla, three tiers arranged on one level from small to large, the only dessert she knew how to prepare. And it was entirely inappropriate because Lorrie had baked a birthday cake.

"At least you know what to expect from her," said Karen.

For Christmas, Gloria stuck a hat on the smallest tier, added buttons and a frosted broom, and called it a snowman. For the Easter egg hunt she'd decorated with floppy ears and jellybeans. Voilà! Bunny! Now the same recipe made a sad third appearance adorned with a screaming "O" for a mouth and matching eyes. A mournful ghost for a children's party.

"Dismal," said Lorrie. "This is why I didn't want to invite her. She's a one-cake mommy. With maroon hair."

"At least she baked," said Karen. "I'll give her ten points for that. Rita's cookies are from Starbucks. I bet she raided the display case when she went out for a morning latte."

Lorrie laughed. Karen was the only mom on Endless Vista who could make her laugh. Both women had put their careers on hold to raise children. Together they planned group treks to Disneyland several times a year, hosted holiday parties, and volunteered for Girl Scout bake sales.

The two women moved with their coffee cups to the sliding doors and gazed out at the wide expanse of lawn. On the other side of the glass were fifteen children, six women, and Gordon, whom Lorrie and Karen had dubbed King of Dads. Gordon was a widower raising his daughter Kimmy under the watchful eyes and approving murmurs of the neighborhood mommies.

"I wish my dad had been like Gordon," Karen said.

"He's taking Kimmy to yoga class now," Lorrie murmured approvingly. "So sweet."

"So sweet."

They sipped coffee. One of the moms waved and Lorrie waved back. She noted the clouds were shifting again from sea blue to gray. There was enough space in the den to move the party indoors if it rained, but she preferred to keep the kids outdoors.

"Scrubs are such a good idea," said Karen.

"Am I a genius? I thought a theme would solve the Rita issue."

In a corner of the yard, near the deserted playhouse, Frances and Annie stood next to one another. Annie held her witch hat in one hand and inclined her head toward Frances, whispering in the younger child's ear.

"Thank you," Karen said, "I couldn't take another one of her forty-year-old cheerleader performances. That was so embarrassing last New Year's! Doesn't Gordon look adorable wearing a stethoscope?"

"I know," Lorrie said, waving through the glass at the King of Dads. "Granted, Rita's scrubs are a size too small, but at least the cleavage is under control."

"Progress has been made and duly noted. Although it does look a little like a doctor's office out there."

Both women laughed.

At 3:00 Lorrie presented the birthday cake. She was especially proud of the centerpiece, a pretty porcelain doll with huge eyes, wearing an exact replica of her daughter's dress.

"Oh, that's perfect!" Karen said, prompting a round of compliments from the other moms.

"Nice work, Lorrie!"

"You're amazing!"

"Look at that little doll! She looks just like you, Frances!"

Only Frances seemed disappointed. She stared silently at the cake, until Annie whispered in her ear. At that, Frances grinned and the two girls linked arms.

The phrase 'thick as thieves' ran through Lorrie's mind. She was ashamed to admit she was jealous of a child, so she smiled broadly and urged Frances to blow out the candles.

"Make a wish! Make a wish!" The kids chanted.

Frances took one last look at Annie in her Goth get-up. Then she closed her eyes and blew out the candles.

After cake and ice cream the grownups relaxed and the kids got jumpy. There was a minor scuffle when Hansel and Gretel told Rita's son Fred he was too fat to be Spider-Man. The boy picked up a Frisbee and hit Gretel in the face with it.

"Little jerk," Karen said under her breath. She went to break up the fight.

"You keep an eye on things, okay?" Lorrie said. "I'm going to wash my hands."

"Sure," said Karen.

A few minutes later Lorrie was studying her face in the bathroom mirror. She had never considered Botox before but the lines emerging across her forehead were more pronounced than the last time she'd paid attention. Maybe Kirk was right. Maybe it was time to go back to an office job. Her daughter would be fine. Wasn't that the whole point of all this effort? To raise a child who could face the world on her own?

The doorbell rang. Lorrie decided to let Karen see to it. Anyone showing up this late didn't deserve a personal greeting from the hostess. A few seconds later she heard Frances call out.

"Welcome to my party!"

Lorrie had to give Karen credit. She knew how to follow rules. Even in Lorrie's absence her friend had made a point of including Frances in the greeting. And for once the child sounded like she was enjoying herself.

Lorrie dried her hands and wandered out to the kitchen. Her coffee cup stood on the counter, where she'd left it. She took a sip while she watched the party on the lawn. She smiled and held up the cup in salute when Karen caught her eye.

"Thanks!" She called out.

"For what?" Karen mouthed with exaggeration.

"The door," Lorrie said, pointing toward the front of the house.

Karen stared blankly at her. Then she shrugged.

Gordon had organized the children into a friendly game of freeze-tag, pulling in even the shy stragglers, all except Frances and Annie, who stood near the back fence watching and smirking. Lorrie noted with a rush of irritation that the girls had exchanged headgear. Frances wore the pointed black hat while Annie had topped off her Goth witch outfit with the ruby-studded silver crown tilted at a rakish angle.

It was all Lorrie could do not to dash outside and tear the crown from the girl's head. She stood perfectly still behind the patio door, breathing. She counted from one to ten, and back, and then started again. She had to do this several times. The numbers began to glide naturally into a head count.

Idly, all afternoon, Lorrie had been keeping track of the number of children and parents. It was a habit. Frances was popular enough to drag friends along on a lot of their excursions. Lorrie frequently found herself counting heads. Even when they were in the car or the living room, she was always running a quick tally.

Her mind registered that something was off. Karen had joined the parents outdoors, so now there were eight moms, fifteen kids and Gordon. But that didn't seem right. Thinking she must have stupidly included herself, Lorrie started with Karen and counted the moms again: Eight. Excluding herself, she counted eight. But there had been six before Karen went outside. Not seven.

Then she remembered the doorbell. Of course, another set of guests had arrived while she was in the bathroom.

"I wonder," said Karen as she returned to the kitchen and picked up her coffee cup, "is it better to make them behave politely, or teach them to be honest and break the news to Fred about his weight problem? Don't answer. I know I'm a monster. I shouldn't be allowed near children, right?"

As she started counting heads again, Lorrie made a discovery. All of the children were accounted for, but there was one adult she didn't recognize.

"Who is that woman?" Lorrie asked.

"Which?"

"Over there. The woman with dark hair."

A woman in scrubs was pulling one of the boys aside,

asking him something. The boy, Charlie, was dressed as a pirate. After a second Charlie responded to the woman by holding up his right hand, fingers splayed.

"Oh," said Karen. "I don't know."

The woman's costume was the only one that looked authentic. In place of the pristine blue and green surgical scrubs the other parents wore, hers were sagging and threadbare and, most alarming, decorated with blood-red stains. Her hair wasn't brushed properly. Above the green surgical mask her eyes were opaque, without expression.

"Didn't you let her in a little while ago?"

"No," said Karen. "I didn't let anyone in. Why? Don't you know her?"

"I've never seen her," said Lorrie.

The woman was crouching next to Frances and Annie. Frances turned at an angle and the woman ran her fingertips over the girl's translucent pink wings. Whatever the woman was saying, the girls appeared to be enraptured.

"What the hell," Lorrie said.

"I don't get it. Why is she dressed like that if she wasn't invited?"

Both women set aside their coffee and went outside. They made a show of not panicking as they strode across the lawn, greeting familiar kids and neighbors along the way. When Lorrie reached the woman, who was still talking to her daughter, she stopped. Frances was holding up six fingers toward the woman. Lorrie gently moved her little girl aside and stepped in front of her.

Annie and Frances wandered away. The woman stood up. She was a bit taller than Lorrie and thinner, with a rangy look to her limbs, as though she hiked a good deal.

"How do you do?" Lorrie said. "I don't think we've met. Did, uh, did one of the other parents invite you?"

The woman nodded.

Karen caught up and introduced herself. Lorrie gave Karen a scorching glance.

"Who would that be?" Lorrie asked. "Who invited you?"

The woman pointed vaguely across the lawn where the children were starting to wind down from their game. She murmured something indecipherable behind her surgical mask, which Lorrie could now see was bloodstained like the rest of her outfit.

"Excuse me," said Lorrie. "I didn't catch your name."

The woman murmured again. This time it sounded like she said, "Anya."

Lorrie noticed a rank odor. It reminded her of the time the garbage disposal had backed up the day after Kirk tried to run steak leftovers through it. She wondered if one of the kids had arrived with dog poop on their shoes, but she hadn't been aware of the smell when she was greeting guests at the front door. She scanned the lawn and saw nothing unusual.

"So, which brat is yours?" Karen asked the woman with the mask.

The woman mumbled and looked away. The odor grew stronger. And now it didn't smell like a garbage disposal.

Lorrie had only encountered such an awful, rotten, yet embarrassingly human scent once. She had been standing in line at a pizza joint in Santa Ana when she smelled something that killed her appetite. The source was a bald teenager with her arms covered in tattoos and a head wound that looked like someone had tried to kill her with an axe. Despite several dozen stitches, the wound in the back of the teenager's head had begun seeping, clearly infected.

"Which one is yours?" Karen asked again.

The masked woman turned toward the crowd of children. Searching. Her eyes clouded and she shook her head.

"She," the woman said through the mask. "She. She!"

The woman looked around the yard and back toward the house.

"Listen," said Lorrie. "I'm not sure how you got in, but…"

Before she could finish, the woman stepped past her. She made a beeline for the sliding glass doors and slipped inside the house so quickly and smoothly, Lorrie was stunned. It took her a moment to come to her senses and follow the woman.

"What the hell just happened?" Karen asked, trailing along after Lorrie.

"I have no idea," Lorrie said over her shoulder, controlling her nerves so she wouldn't ruin the party. "Gordon! Sorry to bug you. Could you come here for a second?"

Gordon caught up with them inside. The hall extended from the front door to the back of the house. Along the hallway an arch gave way to the kitchen and another to the living room, a door led to a half bathroom, and two sets of stairs led up to the bedrooms and down to the den.

"What's up?" Gordon asked.

"There's a strange woman here," said Lorrie.

She inched along, wondering which way to go next, for the woman had slipped out of sight. The last glimpse of her had been a shadow cast on the floor of the hall, followed by the sound of footsteps on stairs.

"Strange how?"

"As in we don't know her," Karen said. "Right, Lorrie? You don't know her? Maybe we should call the police."

"Oh, I think we can handle this," Gordon said. "The kids are outside and it looks like we've got her cornered. How did she get in?"

"I don't know," Lorrie told him. She had to control the growing irritation in her voice. "I thought Karen let her in."

"I didn't," said Karen. "I've never seen her before."

"She must be crazy," said Gordon. "Why would anyone give up a Saturday to hang around with kids who aren't theirs?"

"It isn't really funny," Lorrie told him.

"No, it isn't," said Gordon. "Of course not."

"She smells." This just popped out. Even as she said it, Lorrie felt silly.

"She smells?" Gordon asked. "Of what?"

This was a question Lorrie couldn't fully answer without describing the scene she remembered from the pizza place. The thought turned her stomach.

"Sick," she told them. "Didn't you notice it, Karen?"

"No, but I didn't get very close to her. What do you think it was?"

"Something rank. Gordon, will you go down to the den and look around? Check the closets down there, too. Karen and I can look upstairs."

"Sure," said Gordon. "Stay together."

"Is that a joke?" Lorrie asked.

"No," Gordon said with a solemn face. "Of course not."

"Maybe she's homeless," said Karen. "Or one of those women you read about, who steals kids."

"Let's not get worked up," said Gordon. "I think we can handle this. We can call the police later if you think it's necessary. Right now we need to find her."

Lorrie drew a sharp breath. She trotted up the stairs to the bedrooms with Karen in tow. The floral opulence of the master bedroom prompted Karen to say, not for the first time, "Lorrie, I love your sense of style."

"Thanks," Lorrie replied. "Let's stay focused, okay?"

"Sorry." Karen said. "Okay. Where do we go first?"

Lorrie considered the drapes. She took up a position on one side and Karen stood opposite. Simultaneously they yanked back the curtains. Nothing.

Next they rifled through the closet. Then Lorrie got down on the carpeted floor and crept toward the bed. She reached carefully and pinched a corner of the bed skirt. She heard Karen gasp when she pulled the skirt aside. Nothing.

In the bathroom Lorrie was the one who checked the shower. Karen gasped again, and Lorrie asked, "Are you doing that on purpose?"

"No," said Karen. She held up her hands. "Of course not."

When they were satisfied the woman wasn't hiding in the master bedroom or the bath they moved on. They surveyed every inch of the upstairs. But they found nothing. They even rummaged through the linen closet. That was when Lorrie heard the unmistakable sound of children in the hallway below: stamping feet and shrieks followed by an outburst of giggles. She hurried back downstairs.

Gordon stepped up from the den just as Lorrie and Karen returned to the main floor. He shook his head.

"I checked the den, the closets, everything," he reported.

"I don't understand," said Karen. "We were right behind her."

"Who let the kids into the house?" Lorrie asked.

She heard the front door slam shut. She moved fast, dodging manic kids and stray balloons, to see if the woman was making her escape. Instead she found Frances with her back against the door, dressed from head to toe in Annie's witch costume. For a moment, in her anger and confusion, she forgot about the woman.

"What are you doing with Annie's dress?" Lorrie said.

"I can wear it now," Frances told her.

"Children!" Lorrie shouted. "Outside, right now."

Karen began to herd the kids toward the patio doors. Gordon lingered near Lorrie as though he didn't know what to do next. Out back the other moms stood on the lawn, drinking punch and chatting, ignoring the excitement indoors.

Once the children moved away, Lorrie opened the front door. There was no one on the front lawn or the sidewalk.

"Frances," Lorrie said. "What did that woman say to you a little while ago?"

"Which...?"

"You know which one, the lady who was talking to you and Annie."

Frances giggled.

"What's so funny?"

"She asked how old I am."

"What did you say?"

"This many."

Frances held up her right hand, fingers splayed. With the left she was grasping something, and she had trouble freeing her index finger.

"Did she tell you anything else?"

"She said I had to be seven."

Lorrie and Gordon looked at one another. Then Lorrie's gaze drifted automatically to the back yard, through the glass. She could see Gloria wandering among the children, searching for her daughter. And without even trying, Lorrie began to count...

Ten... eleven... twelve...

"Annie!" Gloria called out.

"She had to go now but she'll be back when I get bigger," Frances said.

Thirteen... fourteen....

"Next year," Frances continued. She opened her left hand so that Lorrie could see what she was holding. In the center of her daughter's palm a small, human tooth glistened with ruby-red spit and a bit of pink gristle.

Lorrie opened her mouth to ask another question. But she was interrupted by a sharp, shrill sound from outdoors. It might have been the children playing, or a woman screaming.

Author's Note: S.P. Miskowski

I find obsessed individuals fascinating. So you could say I'm obsessed with obsession. When someone loses perspective over a compulsive need, the result makes excellent material for fiction.

More personally I'm drawn to stories about family. Our ideas and ideals surrounding family tend to dominate our awareness. We seldom see the damage done by our good intentions. So I like to look closely at relationships steeped in social mythology, to examine gaps between what we want and what we say we want, and between what we say we want and the result of our actions.

JP

Brent Michael Kelley

Waiting in line at the bank, a fire truck drives by. No lights or sirens, so it's not on its way to a catastrophe. That's when the idea hits me... what if that old oak next to the driveway fell on the house? I have this vision of your cage, peeking out from a pile of debris. I see firemen clearing rubble to secure gas lines. I see me and Mommy crying against each other as firemen dig you out of the pile.

I'm starting to sweat and breathe heavy. I feel like a monster for locking you up like a dog.

The teller asks, "Are you all right?"

For some reason, I growl at her. "Just give me the deposit receipt."

Her expression says I just reached in through the little speaker box and slapped her face.

I apologize immediately, say something about being late for a meeting, and speed toward home. My white-knuckled hands grip the steering wheel as I lean forward in the driver's seat. The notion of getting stopped by a cop never occurs to me.

When I get home, the tree hasn't fallen. The house isn't on fire. Everything is fine.

I open your cage, and you climb out happily. You stretch your legs, yawn, and ask me to pick you up. I make you a peanut butter sandwich with the crust cut off, just like you like.

JP, my heart breaks every time I look into your big,

shiny eyes. I brush your hair back so I can see them better, and a lump rises in my throat. I smooth your sweater back to read the words *Daddy's Lil' Monster*. You're a good looking fella, JP. We're two peas in a pod, but you know that.

I lift you up onto my lap and tuck you inside my shirt. It's the only way I can get any work done. It's the only way to get you to stop your adorable whining. You keep my lap and belly warm. You stick your happy face out the neck hole of my t-shirt and kiss me on the cheek. This is how it ought to be, and as far as I'm concerned, we can stay like this forever.

~

Let's face it, JP, doctors are fallible. Dr. Goodhue is no exception, so let's not be too hard on him, okay? I won't go so far as to call him a fraud, but I lost all faith in him today. The man has no idea what he's talking about. What it is, he probably got you confused with someone else he'd seen today. Sometimes people have bad brain days, that's all.

"Enjoy what little time you and JP have left together," he said. "I wouldn't have expected him to live as long as he has."

Well, don't you worry, pal. We won't be seeing Dr. Goodhue again. He doesn't know you, he doesn't know me, and he doesn't know what we can do together.

Let's go for a walk and forget about that poor, confused man.

~

I'm sorry, JP. I know all this furniture moving makes you uncomfortable. Up the stairs, down the stairs, up the stairs, down the stairs. I promise, I'm almost done.

And I know I've been mad all day. I'm not mad at you, I promise. Other people, mostly. Like Dr. Goodhue. That lying douche has been under my skin the last couple days, all because he got his patients mixed up in his head last week. As soon as you're feeling better, we'll go back there and rub your good health in his face.

To be honest, I'm also pretty mad at Mommy for listening to Dr. Goodhue's erroneous assessment. I said some things I shouldn't have. You can help me apologize to her when she gets home from work.

See, Mommy wants me to haul this stuff out to the garage, and I should probably listen to her. She's mad at me for saying mean things, and also for having the tree service cut down all the trees in our yard. It was a little more expensive than I thought it'd be, but that's okay. Now we don't have to worry about them falling on the house when you're home alone.

And I know you were scared when the men came to cut down our trees, pal. That was a lot of noise in the yard, but it was all worth it.

I wish you'd stay out from under foot while I'm carrying heavy things down the stairs, though. I didn't mean to yell, okay? Just, please stay out of the way, okay?

Damn it, JP! *Move!*

JP!

Ahh... AHH!

No... JP... Get away, damn you!

JP, I'm dizzy. I landed on my head, buddy. I think something's broken. My head... my ass... I think something's seriously broken.

Are you okay, JP?

Yesss.

Where are you going? Don't leave, don't leave! I didn't mean to swear at you.

JP?

~

Dr. Mathe says I have a hairline fracture on the top of my

skull and a severely bruised tailbone, JP. He says I can come home to you in two more days. I'm in a lot of pain, but only because you aren't with me. If you were here, you'd shine the pain away like the sun shines away the night.

Mommy brought me a big framed picture of you to sit next to my bed. My visitors and the nurses all ask about you. You're very popular, JP.

I've been sitting on an ice pack since I arrived at St. Stupid's Hospital for Losers. I've got another ice pack on top of my head.

My lap itches where you should be sitting.

Why did I have to be so stupid-clumsy and fall down the stairs?

Just two more days, JP. Two more days of fake smiles. Two more days of listening to nurses tell me about their mangy dogs and disgusting cats. Two more days of acting like I'm in pain from a bruised tailbone or a cracked skull when I'm really just missing you.

I'm so sorry I yelled at you, JP. I'm going to make it up to you, I promise. As soon as I get home, we're going to start going to the park for an hour every day, okay? We'll both be back to our old selves in no time.

~

I didn't get it at the time, but I do now, JP. It took me getting injured to see you in a new light. Limping along behind you in the park, I finally see you're not as peppy as you used to be. You used to dart after squirrels and birds. You used to sprint in wide circles around me. Today, you trot gingerly a little ways before slowing to a walk.

Could Dr. Goodhue have been right after all? The idea sends a painful throb from my tailbone to the top of my head.

I'm sorry, JP.

I knowww.

I'm the guy crying on his knees in the park. Thanks for

letting me hold you. Everyone is looking at us, but I don't care. I don't want to imagine life without you. I refuse to. If there's a way to fix you, I swear I'll find it.

You willll.

~

I haven't slept lately, JP. How could I? I love you.

My head hurts most of the time. The Vicodin only helps so much. It makes me sleepy, but it doesn't put me under. I feel like a zombie. I feel like the world's most helpless monster.

It's 4 a.m., and all I can do is sit at my desk staring at my lap. You should be sitting here. I should go upstairs and get you. No, no. I have to let you sleep. You deserve to rest, snuggled up against Mommy's side.

I look at the stairs, hoping to see you. You're not there.

These medical websites are useless for what I need to find. Useless.

With my head in a fog, I can't focus on the words that fill my screen. I find myself, instead, going through all my pictures of you. There's the one of you jumping up for a treat from Mommy. There's you and your brother Mo wearing matching sweaters. There's one of you sitting on my lap, under my shirt. Your head is sticking out the neck hole, and you're giving me kisses. Both of our faces are content. That's how it should be, you know?

Yesss.

I look to the stairs again, and there you are. Come here, pal. Jump up on my lap where you belong.

Alwaysss.

JP, my head hurts.

Sooon.

I don't want anything to happen soon, JP! I want things to stay this way!

Trussst meee.

I... I understand. I know what you want me to do.

Beee ssstrong.

I will. God, my head hurts, JP. I can barely think.

~

We did it, JP. We did it.

Lying on the floor, I can't feel you moving. I can't feel anything, JP. Seems I lost more blood than I thought I would. It doesn't matter. Nothing matters but you.

I've never stitched a wound before. I should have studied up on that a little more. Fishing line, JP! If you had told me a week ago I'd be using fishing line to sew up a—

"Jesus Christ!" a man screams.

My drowsy eyes float over to the door where my neighbor Mr. Cook has let himself in. He doesn't notice his comb-over hairdo dancing over his head, but we do, don't we JP? I only know his last name from his mailbox, and I don't have a clue what his first name is. He doesn't know us well enough to come into our house uninvited, JP.

"I heard you screaming," he says. He looks like he wants to puke. "What... what did you *do?*"

"Please..." I say. My voice is weak. I reach a trembling hand toward him. "Please..."

"I'm getting an ambulance," he blurts. His hand dives into his pocket, and pulls out an antique-looking cell phone. He fumbles with it— a true warrior of the digital revolution.

"No... wait," I tell him. My voice is even weaker. I gesture for him to come close.

His eyes dart from my stomach, to his phone, to my eyes, to the blood pooling beneath me. He looks at you, JP, and he covers his mouth.

I swallow my rage. I force myself to forgive him. He doesn't know anything about anything, the nosy bastard. If he can't see you for the beautiful creature you are, that's his problem. I won't hold his stupidity against him.

Cook bends down on his creaky old knees. His face is

pale, shocked. His lips tremble as he tries to think of something to say. His hands look like he's playing an imaginary piano as he tries to find a way to help.

I lick my lips, take a deep breath, and open my mouth to speak.

Cook bends down further and turns his head. His ear is so close to my face I could count his bushy ear hairs.

My hand squeezes the grip of the scalpel, and I plunge it into Cook's neck. He makes a choking sound and tries to pull away, but my other hand has him by the shirt. I stick him in the neck again.

Again.

Againnn!

This isn't personal. It's for you, JP. If he called an ambulance, they'd cut you out of me. No one is taking you away from me, JP. You're part of me now.

As Cook kicks around the floor, getting blood all over the tiles, I almost feel bad for him. I feel worse for Mrs. Cook, though. She's bound to notice her husband hasn't been home since he left to see why the neighbor was screaming. Poor Mrs. Cook.

It's all for you, JP.

For usss.

~

I'm glad you slept through that JP. You've had a hard day already, and I can't say the next day will be any better. In fact, I'm certain when our circulatory and nervous systems merge, that's when the real pain will begin.

I wish there was another way, but that's how it has to be. Change is a painful process, but certainly not as painful as letting you go. If I ever had to do that, I couldn't go on.

Skinning you alive was the most painful thing I've ever done, JP. I wish I could have spared you that somehow, but there was no other way. Seeing you naked to the meat from the neck down is a memory I wish I could burn away.

Your face when I held you down— when I peeled your skin— nearly broke my heart.

Things will get harder soon, but not as hard as a lifetime without you. We'll have to run, JP. There's no other way.

Because Mommy will be home from work soon, buddy, and she won't approve of this either. Poor Mommy will try to separate us, too.

Yesss.

One hand holds the scalpel, and the other strokes your mane as we wait. Inside me, I think I can feel your tail wagging. My vision is getting dark and sparkly, JP. It doesn't matter. Nothing does, now that we'll be together...

Foreverrr.

Author's Note: Brent Michael Kelley

JP. He's my little buddy. We brought him home the day after the Green Bay Packers beat the Pittsburgh Steelers in the Super Bowl. He's a dog of the Chinese Crested variety. We have two in my house, the other being Mo. I'm not obsessed with either of them, however.

Last summer I went to South Africa for three weeks. During that time, JP sat on my chair a lot and stared at the door. I showed his picture (Mo's, too) to all my new friends in South Africa, including the chief of Nyetse, a village up toward Botswana. I know I was missed while I was away, and I doubt anyone missed me more than JP. I am, however, not obsessed with that dog.

JP sits on my lap under my shirt a lot while I write. Like right now. He sits there snoozing and keeping my belly warm— the strangest good luck charm I presently have. I guess he makes sure I write good or stuff. Sometimes I have to go to the bathroom or I need a refill on my coffee, but I sit there and press on because I don't want to disturb JP. Since you bring it up, I'll add that I'm not obsessed with JP.

JP is always happy. He always has kisses for me. He loves to play fetch with me. He barks with joy when I come home from a twenty minute trip to town. I think *he* might be a little obsessed with *me*. It's interesting that I'll be able to sew him into my body if he ever shows any signs of aging (which won't be for at least another 50 or 60 years) so that we can live together forever as one creature. But no, I wouldn't say I have an obsession.

Good ol' JP...

Kestrel

Mary Borsellino

Her parents named her Kestrel, because bird names were the fashion. When she was twelve years old she discovered that the name came from the old French word for rattle, after the sound the bird made.

Another child might have found that funny, considering. But then again if she'd been another child, it wouldn't have been funny.

If she'd been another child, she wouldn't be so habitually quiet that her parents forgot she was in the room almost daily, and discussed her with a frankness that nobody should ever hear themselves talked about, especially not by their parents and especially not when they are twelve.

A girl as silent as a shadow, named for a harsh sound. Another child might have found that funny.

Kestrel almost never talked. Years of speech pathology had helped a little, drawn her out of her throat enough that she could get by in public. She liked going to the movies on her own, and sometimes the only thing she'd say for the whole week would be 'one student ticket' at the box office, and then 'no' at the candy bar when they asked if she wanted to supersize.

If her parents or her speech pathologist had heard her, she'd have earned a scolding. It should be 'one student ticket, *please*' and 'no, *thank you*', they'd explain. But without them there to bully her into it, Kestrel excised the extra words and made it all just a fraction easier for herself.

She'd been a quiet, placid baby, almost never crying, content to watch the world around her and play games with her toys. Her parents, not naturally inclined to excessive huggings and cuddlings to begin with, didn't really notice that she rarely reached for them and didn't seem to care one way or another when she was snuggled and kissed.

Kestrel had been an exemplary daughter, in fact, right up until the day when her father had found her sitting among her building blocks on the rug, stacking them up methodically, with blood running in thick dark rivulets down her soft baby chin from her mouth. She'd bitten off the tip of her tongue.

A childhood's worth of tests later, and Kestrel knew these things about herself: she felt no pain. She could tell a kiss from a pinch on her cheek, but beyond pressure and texture there was no difference in the two sensations for her.

When she was seven she ran up a flight of cement stairs too fast, stubbing her toes so hard against one of the steps that three of them broke and one lost its nail. She didn't realise this for two days, until her father saw the crooked, purple digits and swore.

"Jesus, not again."

One of the phrases the doctors used a lot was 'pain is a modifier of actions.' Even though she was a quiet, observant little person, it was still years before Kestrel properly understood what that meant.

She was playing marbles with her brother in the living room one winter day when she was nine and a half. One of the marbles, a grey clambroth, the pride of their collection, bounced against a fold in the rug and skewed unexpectedly, rolling into the unscreened fireplace.

Kestrel reached in to grab it, then looked down in surprise at the dark burns blooming where the skin of her fingers had touched the burning coals.

"Oh," she said, going to the kitchen to retrieve ice from

the freezer.

Her brother, Bertl, yelled loudly for their mother to come quickly. Kestrel tried to shush him, because their parents were getting ready for a party that night and didn't want to be interrupted, but Bertl yelled and yelled.

Kestrel quite liked her little brother, really, but sometimes he was more trouble than he was worth.

"What did you do?" their mother asked as she came into the kitchen, slipping the hook of a long diamond earring into her ear. As always, she was absolutely beautiful, except for the frown on her pretty mouth.

"I put my hand in the fire."

"Christ all mighty. All right, get in the car. We'll have to go to the emergency room."

"I'm sorry."

"It's done now," their mother sighed. She sounded tired and annoyed. "I'll go tell your father."

After that, Kestrel always remembered not to touch the fire. She wondered if that was what the doctors meant about pain modifying actions, or if she'd got things wrong about that, the way she did about everything.

At thirteen, after she knew what her name meant but didn't find it especially funny, Kestrel went to high school and managed to pinch her leg in a door in such a way that the skin split and needed fourteen stitches up her calf.

She forgot that they were there on the school's track and field afternoon, three days later. During the hurdles race she stretched her leg on a leap and all the stitches popped, sending blood gushing down her leg and staining her sock and shoe. The teachers cancelled the rest of the afternoon's activities, and all the other students glared at Kestrel with childish murder in their eyes.

One girl, Adelaide, pulled hard on Kestrel's braid as she walked past her. One of the teachers saw it and sent both the girls into the principal's office.

Ms. Castor, the principal, was angry at them both. Neither of the girls cared much about this fact, which was probably the single thing they had in common with one another.

"What? It's not like it matters. She doesn't feel pain," Adelaide said blithely when Ms. Castor told her she should feel ashamed for bullying Kestrel like that.

"Just because she can't feel physical pain doesn't mean she doesn't have emotions just like yours," Ms. Castor chided with a frown. Adelaide shook her head.

"No she doesn't. Look at her, she's like a robot."

"You have detention for a week. Go get changed out of your sports clothes and go back to class."

So ordered by the principal, Adelaide left. Kestrel wondered if ordinary people could feel it when someone radiated hatred, the way Adelaide had. Kestrel couldn't feel it, only sense it through Adelaide's actions and words. She wondered what it felt like. Was it like temperature, or texture? She knew those things, in the broadest of terms.

"Kestrel," Ms. Castor sighed. "I'm worried about you."

Kestrel looked down at her leg, which was still bleeding. Her sock and shoe hadn't started leaking on the floor, though, luckily. It always caused trouble when she made a mess.

"Don't worry, it doesn't hurt," she replied.

"That's not..." Ms. Castor sat beside her. "You have to be careful of yourself. If a cut like this got infected, you could get very sick."

Kestrel shrugged. "So?"

Ms. Castor looked at her, like she was searching for something in Kestrel's face. Kestrel was used to people doing that. She just stared back, and waited until Ms. Castor gave up.

Eventually, Ms. Castor sighed and stood up. "Come on. Let's go to the nurse's office and get that cleaned up."

While the nurse washed her leg and put a dressing on the cut and wrapped a bandage around to keep the dressing in place, Kestrel sat and listened to Ms. Castor fight with Kestrel's mother on the telephone.

"...can feel empathy, and sadness. Her flat affect has nothing to do with her condition. It's just that she's a profoundly unhappy child," Ms. Castor said angrily.

Kestrel looked down at her leg, watching as the nurse methodically wound the length of bandage around and around. Even Ms. Castor, who was saying something so compassionate, was still talking about her like she wasn't there. She was a little ghost, haunting her own life.

She started skipping school so that she could go to the movies more often. She liked sitting in the dark and watching other people. It was what she was best at.

Kestrel liked the way movies built stories, how interactions were constructed. It wasn't like how people related to one another in real life. In the movies, everything that every character said was something the writer had thought about, and put in there on purpose. It wasn't like the real world at all, where people hardly ever thought about what they said and would say things without caring in the least whether their little girl was in the room and could hear them.

From the movies, she started to learn other things that nobody had thought to teach her: when people, ordinary people, felt terribly depressed, they didn't feel as much pain. When they were having sex, pain didn't seem to work in the same way as it did at other times.

When she was sixteen, she tried having sex a few times, to see if she could feel that. The boys got uncomfortable when she asked them to do it harder, to make her bruise. After a while she gave up trying.

Maybe it would have been different, she thought, if she did it with someone she cared about, instead of someone who wasn't important. But caring was dangerous, one of the very few things in all the world which threatened true pain if it went wrong.

She was seventeen when Ms. Castor gave her the details of a student script writing contest.

"You're truant at the movies so often, you might as well

put what you've learned to good use and make a movie of your own. But you'll have to give yourself a broader knowledge base first. Those shitty action flicks you love have skewed what you know about how much things hurt, what real reactions are like."

Kestrel wanted to tell her that for every two hours she might spend watching *Die Hard* or its ilk, she'd watched twenty-two hours of real people doing real things as well. But instead she just shrugged.

So at Ms. Castor's insistence she watched a slew of classics and art house movies and recorded plays. Despite what she was meant to be learning from them, Kestrel found that she liked the silent movies the best. Without sound at their disposal, the film-makers had been forced to create a different language to tell the audience what the characters were thinking and feeling. Kestrel liked their exaggerated, monochrome faces, their theatrical gestures.

After she'd watched enough movies to get an idea for her own, Kestrel turned off the television and sat down at her keyboard and started to write.

If she'd been a different girl, she might have found the whole thing funny, the idea of someone who couldn't feel anything trying to make other people feel something. But if she'd been a different girl, there wouldn't have been anything funny about it. She was just herself, just the girl with the bird-name and scars on her skin.

She finished the script and posted it off to the contest on Monday morning. Ms. Castor wanted to see a copy, but Kestrel refused to show her. If it didn't win the contest, she wasn't going to let anyone else see it. She might not know when her toes were broken, but this injury at least would be one that she'd be able to keep private.

It came second place. Which wasn't quite a win, but wasn't quite a failure either, and in the face of this ambiguity Kestrel decided to let Ms. Castor read the entry.

Her script was the story of a ghost, a girl made of nothing but shadow. She tried to be a part of the world but it never worked out the way she wanted it to. People complained when she tried to get close to them, because she'd block the light and make it hard for them to read, or make photographs turn out badly if she tried to attend gatherings and parties.

The shadow-girl never spoke or made any other noise. All her thoughts and emotions were conveyed through body language alone, a silhouette having to do all the work of dialog and expression both. There seemed no way for her to be a part of the world, until one of the other characters gave her a book of braille, which the ghost-girl could read by skimming her shadow over the little bumps, changing their tiny cast of light just enough with the movement for her to understand.

"It should have won first place," Ms. Castor said loyally, after reading it. Kestrel shrugged.

"It's okay. I'll do better next time."

"Oh?" Ms. Castor's voice was cautiously arch. "You're going to enter again next year."

"Maybe," Kestrel answered, shrugging one of her shoulders a second time. "Or I might just make one on my own."

"You've learned that you don't need someone else to tell you something's good in order for you to know it has worth, then?"

"If you wanted me to learn this big life lesson about opinions being wrong or whatever, you could have just told me that, you know," Kestrel said in her usual deadpan voice.

Ms. Castor shook her head. "No, I couldn't."

Kestrel nodded. "Yeah, I guess I know that. People can only learn if the lesson's in a language they know, right? But how did you know that I'd know this one, that I'd understand something I learned from writing scripts?"

That made Ms. Castor smile. "Oh, that's easy. It's because there's no such thing as painless art."

Author's Note: Mary Borsellino

When I was a kid I went through many phases of ambition— I want to be a doctor! I want to be a hairdresser! I want to be a detective!— the same as anyone else at that age. The difference with me was that I assumed that when everyone else said things like that, they meant it the same way I did, which was "I want to write books and be a doctor! I want to write books and be a hairdresser!" and so on. It genuinely never occurred to me that this wasn't simply a baseline fact of existence. Being alive meant wanting to tell stories. The rest was variables, but that was immutable, wasn't it?

Now, as an adult, I know with my head that this isn't the case, that a lot of people— most people, even— don't feel that absolute drive to tell stories no matter what. But I don't know it with my heart. I never will. I can't imagine what it would be to wake up and not care about making up things and sharing them with people. And since I'm pretty sure that anything which tilts the axis of your life to that degree is an obsession, I guess we'll have to call it that.

An Unattributed Lyric, In Blood, On a Bathroom Wall

Ennis Drake

"...he did not fling away life with precipitate haste,

but... according to his humour."

—Tacitus, *The Annals*

Everything ends, in its way. Just as all things are Eternal, in their way. Lives may end, but the genes carry on through our children and grandchildren— those ever-extending branches of heredity, that great sum of biological process; memories are carried on, in the minds and hearts of friends, loved ones, enemies, tiny fragments of US, sacred even in death, living even in death, simply because we have been loved or hated, because we have touched, challenged, influenced, or inspired. Perhaps it feels to you as if I've opened with a digression. Perhaps it is best to not openly wonder (now) at the nature of immortality (such as it is). Maybe it is good enough to say: To have an end is a blessing. To have an end is, if not to have resolution, then, at least, to have stillness. Cessation is peace.

This is the Beginning. This is a character, in a situation. As you will (or, so I hope) very shortly agree, his name is unimportant, a point further made by the use of the 2nd person narrative— the effect, the *intention*, being *summa habitationem*. Exposition: A restaurant. You could find two score just like it in any city in North America. Once, it might really have been 'Family-Owned.' Hell, maybe it still is. Maybe the ambiguously ethnic guy in the rolled sleeves and suit vest has a less ambiguous familial tie to the folks who opened the doors in 1989 (Greek, Slav, Turk? Definitely Mediterranean, because the food's Mediterranean, you might reason, except the Mexicans running the kitchen put a lid on that pigeon hole, don't they? There's certainly no room for speculation among the wait staff: too varied, save the manner of the pairing of their X's [XX] and D's [DD]. Whoever does the hiring is a tit-man, and it's not the Mediterranean Ken doll who is as gay as he is gorgeous). You watch as he moves from the wait station to the kitchen, to the bar, to the hostess stand. You wonder how his American Dream has turned out, imagining him as you do in the black Corvette C6 parked out front, an image that, were there not a now-marked lack of blood in your body, has its potential for arousal. You don't get skin that smooth, that flawless, at that age without a good dermatologist, and you can't afford a good dermatologist (microdermabrasion, acid peel, laser rejuvenation) working in a restaurant unless you're taking in a percentage right off the top. The vest and the slacks are tailored. The shirt: probably not. What does it mean?

It doesn't mean anything, of course. Except as an example of career choices that were smarter than yours.

"That's a long fucking list," you mumble.

"What's that? The people you've pissed off?"

You make an involuntary sound; it's neither laugh nor grunt.

"Listen, I've got a long one ahead of me. It's a three-hour drive. I hope you're feeling at least marginally better," your companion says, wiping his mouth on the cotton napkin that's been sitting in his lap. Mouth clean, he wads the napkin and tosses it on top of his plate, which, unlike yours, has been clear for a while.

Your forearms are open beneath your coat. The rubber hosing, not to mention the wounds themselves, have made your arms numb below the elbow. You can't feel the blood running out onto the carpet.

"Yeah. Yeah, you better get going," you say, staring at the soiled cloth on top of the fossils of your friend's dinner.

It's hard to look at him. His face shows clearly the mingling of regret, annoyance, and an impatience to be gone. You don't blame him. Your face has looked the same in every mirror you've looked into since you were at least sixteen. In truth, you'd rather be alone. There is to be no light and playful verse for your ears, or the eschewing of the nature of mortality. Just the amalgam din of diners and dates and drowning men at the bar, and the damning voice between your ears. This is what you think about when you've gone to eat your own Last Supper with the Lone Apostle (the only one of your peers that'll still talk to you).He's a big man, your friend— 6' 4", 350 lbs. of muscle and grit— a fact you've always found incongruous with his considerable mind and talent. God knows why. Social programming at work, you suppose. But it *is* the abutment of these traits that has always reminded you of Bob Salvatore, who famously said that when he needed inspiration to write, he taped a copy of his mortgage statement to his computer monitor.

The seat creaks, groans, as the booth gives birth to him, as the haunted house of the world creaks and groans when its door opens to accept us in at the moment of our earthly genesis. You realize as you watch him go— this man who's achieved less critical success than yourself, a man more dedicated to his craft, and certainly more deserving of accolades, this man who earned your admiration from the very beginning— that your friendship has found and exceeded the limits of his extraordinary patience. You always knew he'd be the last to go. But you knew he'd go.

He doesn't look back.

The restaurant is dark, the corner booth at the back darkest of all... and nearest to the bathrooms. The wall sconces are dialed back; just as orange and illy luminous as the candles on the tables; diffuse and wholly evocative of the lobby of whatever Hell awaits.

You laugh. You can't help it. People stare, forks stopping in mid-stroke, scraping to a halt, hanging in mid-air. You're thirty-nine years old and you're still not sure whether you *believe* in Hell.

At that moment, surety: It's all been for nothing.

That's the secret of life; it's the same as the secret dread of the faithful: It really is about nothing. All of it. The work and its companion suffering, that agonizing false hope that was the chemical compound of ego and insecurity? *All for fucking nothing.* There's no such thing as immortality through art. Everything rots. Everything dies. Even the universe is going to stop expanding one day. Then what?

This is the Middle. The Rising Action. The Dark Heart of the story; Drama, absent Resolution; the special place where tailored suspense meets expectation... and they *dance*. This is where we explore, exposit, *expose* the mystery of the rubber hoses. I give to you the death of Petronius, according to Tacitus (according to Jonny Diamond of L Magazine):

"Yet he did not fling away life with precipitate haste, but having made an incision in his veins and then, according to his humour, bound them up, he again opened them, while he conversed with his friends, not in a serious strain or on topics that might win for him the glory of courage. And he listened to them as they repeated, not thoughts on the immortality of the soul or on the theories of philosophers, but light poetry and playful verses."

Your phone dings in your coat pocket. You've learned to loathe that sound. To hate it with every slowly-dying fiber in your body for all that it is not, has not been, cannot be.

An e-mail from your agent:

PS Publishing passed on the proposal.

I'm sorry. We'll reorganize and move on to some smaller houses that might be more receptive.

Yours,

B.

You're cold, your blood-pressure has dropped, your heart slowed. The restaurant spins right, then left, left, left. The group of women at the table near your booth treble in profile, shadow resonances that harken the coming of staid darkness. Stale, black Death is in the hall, silken sack drawn, open and accepting for that weight that measurably leaves the body when the body is of no more use. Conversation becomes an alien buzz punctuated by the occasional baboon warble of laughter, the broken glass sound of silver- and dinnerware, clinking flutes of champagne, and the rattling burdens of busboys clearing tables for the swelling patronage beyond the hostess's single, indefensible cherry palisade.

You shut your eyes.

Snatches of conversation:

"I unfriended her."

"God, Lilliana, you didn't!"

"Did you see what she posted on Instagram?! Oh, God, she just texted me."

You open your eyes.

These are not teenagers. These are women hurriedly approaching fifty: all bone and blonde and red lipstick.

You look into your lap, at your own cotton napkin wadded in your hands. It is dark with blood. Black and sodden with blood. As are the sleeves of your suede coat.

What strange animals we are.

You think briefly of your book (a contemplation of social media, sociopathy, and the collapse of civilization) as you push-pull your way free of the booth. You wonder what will happen to it (you know what will happen to it: it will be lost in the shuffle of popular books by *New York Times* columnists and TV Critics from *Entertainment Weekly* and from there drowned in the flea-market riot of barking small press authors and self-published adherents of the 'Indie Revolution.' You wonder if you have any strength to care, now, now that it's almost done. You suppose you don't. You suppose it's meaningless. As meaningless to you as the *Buğulama* was to the person that cooked, plated, and forgot it as soon as it was given over to you to be consumed.

You retreat to the final sanctuary, pushing through the door marked MEN, legs as numb as your arms.

These... these are the circumstances of your passage. These are the next to final thoughts of a man who has ritually opened his forearms from elbow to wrist with a razor knife, covered them with gauze, and arrested the death sure to follow with two tourniquets fashioned from rubber hose.

This is the End. This is what is scrawled on the bathroom wall in the heart's ink:

"This is my Kingdom Come. This is my Kingdom Come..."

Author's Note: Ennis Drake
Just Another Dead Writer

> "Throw dirt on me
> And grow a wildflower"
> —Dwayne Michael Carter, Jr. (aka Lil' Wayne)

Dead writers have become my obsession of late. Not just dead writers, but suicides[1]. *Felos de se.* Self-murderers. Rope, bullet, buckshot, box-cutter and a tub full of warm water. Throwing themselves, lemming-like, from the bridges of the world. Pockets full of stones in the rocket's red glare.

I take comfort in these extraordinary minds.

I take no comfort in these extraordinarily frail wills.

Dichotomous as my birth sign[2], my comfort/discomfort.

I've held a gun to my head on more than one occasion. Steel pressed tight to the thinning hair at my temple. There's no need for the excessive pressure the hand and arm exert— that bullet's going to do all the digging, man— but you push, you white-knuckle anyway. Call it the manifest struggle of will vs. instinct. *Are you ready to* rock? You just have to (pull the trigger) make the decision: Yes, die/No, live. *It's a shit world, any old way,* you tell yourself. And that's not even factoring the depression[3]. Your panic disorder[4]. Functioning alcoholism. And what's more... dead writers, dead *good* writers, win Nobels, Pulitzers, the Man Booker, the O. Henry. Dead *good* writers sell books. Dead writers, however good or not, are not around to appreciate these things, moldering as they are in their coffins, chalky as they are in their urns, or Maxwell House coffee tins, or wherever the fuck their third or fourth spouse happens to be keeping them. It's a sticking point, the moldering, chalky, coffee-tin thing. Alternatively, you *could* have your ashes fired into the sky in a giant rocket-slash-firework, a great big fiery cock penetrating the Colorado night, at the expense of your dear, dear friend Johnny Depp[5]. You'd be the worst sort of liar to deny the confession: meeting death on your own terms has more than just a little appeal. It's hardly a historically unrecognized human ambition. But even if you reconcile death[6], you must have the work. A legacy[7]. A 'body' to leave behind to be commented on in the context of your corporeal disinvestment. This is— the body of work— as you might have guessed, important.

Which brings me to the central figure of my obsession: David Foster Wallace.

> When David Foster Wallace committed suicide, his death wasn't just mourned— it was read. It was read like code, like apology, like an event in a novel— not simply a plot-level event but a meta-level event, a commentary on the history and future of the novel itself. Insofar as one could find hope in his magnum opus *Infinite Jest*— 'no single moment is unendurable'— his death seemed to negate this hope, to proclaim that this hope was not— ultimately, in the final analysis— enough.
>
> —The Deaths of David Foster Wallace,
>
> Leslie Jamieson, Vice.com

If David Foster Wallace 'killed himself because he'd lost faith in postmodernism and/or his own efforts to replace it; because he was sick of irony but couldn't see a way out of it; because his own virtuosic mind was no match for its own despair...' you realize (I realize) the alternative is not necessarily a return to modernism or romanticism or even an 'oscillation' between detachment and hope, as proposed by the proponents of metamodernism, but to distill the horror in the headlines, on the streets, in our homes; make it pure and objective; naked and starkly-lit; ram it killing, raping, burning, pleading, heartless down the throats of the unsuspecting masses; make them see with the eyes of your overdeveloped sense of empathy (with or without revealing yourself); make them feel every slow-motion moment of horror, hopelessness, revulsion, desperation, resignation; if you can find, together with your reader, true redemption after that, then you have succeeded where Wallace 'failed.' The irony (and perhaps it is an irony upon an irony) is that you cannot find redemption after that. David's failure was in ever believing you could. I have seen no true or lasting redemption in this world and I've seen it at its worst, and at its best. So, you see: and what you see is hatred and despair; the stories you tell are hatred and despair; you live hatred and despair. You (I) have failed from the onset, and *knowingly*. You KNOW that what you are writing is the failure of man, and eventually it will kill you as surely as the inversion killed Wallace. I'll never be a Wallace, not even if I throw all ambition at it, but one thing I can and will be is another dead writer. But I refuse to be *just* another dead writer; without legacy, without the 'body' in whose content my death becomes both context and commentary. So I go on. I keep writing. Don't get me wrong: It's not heroic, but it's not blue-collar, either. It's somewhere between the two. Maybe, when it's all said and done, there's something romantic in that. Maybe, just maybe, there's hope in the act of persisting.

~ ~ ~

[1] In no particular chronological order, I offer: Sylvia Plath, 30; Petronius, 39; Virginia Woolf, 59; Ernest Hemingway, 61; Yukio Mishima, 45; Anne Sexton, 45; Richard

Brautigan, 49; and John Kennedy Toole, 31. The list goes on. It will always go on. And shortly. Elsewhere. Why? I posit simply (and perhaps it is an *over*simplification, but I defy you to challenge my experience): The mind collapses and the body is a prison from which we stare out into the razor-wire bordered expanses of Life.

[2] Gemini. Mutable Air. Here I list celebrities of the same birth sign as a purely superfluous aside: John F. Kennedy, Tupac Shakur, Morgan Freeman, Kanye West, Marilyn Monroe, Angelina Jolie, John Wayne, and Johnny Depp.

[3] After completing *Between the Acts*, Virginia Woolf dressed in her coat, filled the pockets with stones, and drowned herself in the green waters of the Sussex Ouse... but not before she so famously wrote to her husband, Leonard:

Dearest,

I feel certain that I am going mad again. I feel we can't go through another of those terrible times. And I shan't recover this time. I begin to hear voices, and I can't concentrate. So I am doing what seems the best thing to do. You have given me the greatest possible happiness. You have been in every way all that anyone could be. I don't think two people could have been happier 'til this terrible disease came. I can't fight any longer. I know that I am spoiling your life, that without me you could work. And you will I know. You see I can't even write this properly. I can't read. What I want to say is I owe all the happiness of my life to you. You have been entirely patient with me and incredibly good. I want to say that— everybody knows it. If anybody could have saved me it would have been you. Everything has gone from me but the certainty of your goodness. I can't go on spoiling your life any longer. I don't think two people could have been happier than we have been.

V.

[4] Lexapro, Alprazolam, full-figured bitter and expensive Xanax, Nortriptyline, Paxil, Atenolol, Lorazepam. Drugs, drugs, drugs, and it's not even recreational use. No. It's to *live*. Just that. Just to live like a normal person.

[5] We are, of course, talking about Hunter S. Thompson, whose introduction seems unnecessary. Let us instead review his outtro, by way of accounting Ralph Steadman's eulogy. According to Robert Chalmers of GQ Magazine, it went thisly:

> Hunter S. Thompson fucked up my life. He was a bastard. But he was a good bastard. I used to tell him he was a fraud,' Steadman said, recalling Hunter's perennial threats to blow his brains out. 'I am deeply sorry that I was wrong.

It is, however, imo, *most* fitting to examine what Thompson himself wrote after visiting the grave of Ernest Hemingway:

> It's not just a writer's crisis, but they are the most obvious victims because the function of art is supposedly to bring order out of chaos, a tall order even when the chaos is static, and a superhuman task when chaos is multiplying... So finally, and for what he must have thought the best of reasons, he ended it with [his] shotgun.

Thompson, who wrote of 'the dead-end loneliness of a man who makes his own rules.'

[6] Since we're being honest, you and I, I must confess that most of this was written prior to being Baker Acted by my publisher for threatening to eat a bottle of Xanax. Mischief, Mayhem, Want, and Woe, to borrow a phrase.

[7] And so we come to Hemingway himself. We have talked of (or implied) depression, failed marriages, 'the writer's crisis,' suicide, and literary legacies. In the context of soul-deep dissatisfaction, we *must* make further mention of Papa, if only briefly: Four wives; three sons; ten novels, ten short story collections, five works of non-fiction; the Pulitzer; the Nobel Prize in Literature; and one favorite shotgun.

Black Eyes Broken

Mercedes M. Yardley

Natalia broke everything that she touched with any sort of care. Precious things shattered into shards. Glass baubles. Her mother's maternal desires. Hopes. She often stood in the middle of the room, her hands and heart ripped and bloodied, carnage on the floor. She didn't mean to; it was just the way of it.

In the second grade, she kissed a beautiful young boy. He had dark curls and even darker eyelashes, and she knew secretly that he had been born from the sea.

"I like you very much," she whispered, and the kiss was soft and gentle and oh so extraordinary. The boy smiled and then his face cracked and his eyes fell out of his head. Natalia woke up screaming and her mother said it was a dream, only a dream, but the boy didn't come to class the next day. Or the next. Or the next. They found him when the snow thawed, buried in the desert with blooming cactus growing in his empty sockets. He was still lovely, but it was a strange kind of beautiful.

She found a black kitten in high school. Its face was roughed up and his tail broken where she assumed he had been swung over somebody's head. He didn't have any whiskers and most of his fur had been shaved off, but he was a Thing Of Beauty, a Gift From The Universe. He was tiny and afraid and hurt and huddled against her chest when she held him. She fed him milk out of a dropper and told him that she'd always love him, that he was the most wonderful kitty on earth, that she would never, never leave him. She brushed her warm hands against his cold, bare skin and silently begged him never to leave her, either.

She found shreds of skin and fur. Slivers of rib. Blood stains that led to the neighbor's big dog, red foam dripping from his lips.

Natalia closed herself off. Hid in her hoodies and behind black eye-makeup that ran down her face in the rain. She kept to herself so the poison wouldn't be spread, so the death could be held inside and not released by her love. She stayed away from school. Left home on the off-chance that she might eventually grow to love her mother. She seldom spoke. She chose not to read, because reading an author's words often meant falling in love with them.

One day, she met a thin redhead at the store. He scratched at his face and his lips twitched and he was horrifyingly unlovely in his misery and need. The way his eyes followed her, and the way his mouth worked to moisten itself, an unpleasant desert...

Well. Pity is not love.

He came home with her. Offered to carry her groceries and fix the lights the next time they shorted.

"I'll never love you," she warned him. "I don't even want to know your name." She thought he would shuffle his feet, but he didn't. He stood straight and firm and rubbed the sores on his arms.

"I know," he whispered, and his voice was of the wind, of something already gone. Already disappeared. Natalia realized that somebody had breathed him in long ago, taken the most precious parts, and this was what was left. A shell. A shadow.

He never smiled. Not ever, but his lips formed into something that wasn't a frown, not exactly. She didn't exactly frown back.

"Good," she said, and turned off the lights. They watched the broken city struggle and moan far beneath them.

"I loved this city once," she whispered. "You can see what happened."

He slipped his cold hand into hers.

"Not to worry. I'm already broken."

She told herself it wasn't affection. It was necessity. He was heat in the dark of the city, an extra 98.6 degrees and the sound of breaths that made the nights more bearable. That was all.

That was all.

Months later she threw up. She felt hungry and ill and started to care when the redhead didn't come home at night.

"You," she said one evening. Her voice shook as she said it, and she couldn't look him in the eye, although she wanted to. Oh, how she wanted to.

"You," she said again, and they were both trembling by this time. He put his thin arms around her, locking them as tightly as he could bear. As she could bear. He kissed her on her mouth for the first time. Kissed her cheeks and neck and just under her ear. Let his lips linger there. He whispered his name to her.

It was the most perfect thing she had ever heard. She bit her lip and closed her eyes. He touched his forehead to hers and very nearly smiled again. He stepped onto their balcony and jumped.

There was no sound when he fell. There was a sound when he landed, but Natalia tried hard not to think about that. About his red hair running redder. About his heart smashing to pieces. About their baby who twisted and grew and swelled inside her.

Natalia didn't open her eyes. She thought of this wondrous being, this tiny thing, and shattered glasses, black kittens, and precious, precious junkies with lost eyes and red hair. Tears smudged her mascara, made her eyes run black.

She thought of her baby and waited for the cracks.

Author's Note: Mercedes M. Yardley

I once read that writers write in order to discover what their current obsessions are. I didn't realize how true that was until I examined my own work to see what rose to the surface.

I'm obsessed with women in peril. More than that, I'm drawn to women who are boxed into their situations through no fault of their own, but by a whim of the universe. They're fated to be murdered, or fated to break the things they love. They're trapped to say only lovely things when they really want to scream inside. They're born with magic. With curses. With ugliness and beauty. And once they're dealt this hand, how do they cope?

They deal either beautifully or horribly, but they also don't live in a bubble. There are others who are pulled into their lives and are forced to cope with the aftermath. They have friends, family, and lovers who often bend and even break under the weight of their responsibility. I'm obsessed with love and people who try their best in it. I'm obsessed with the broken.

BEARS: A FAIRY TALE OF 1958

Steve Duffy

They tried so hard, the bear family; really they did. They'd known from the get-go there'd be difficulties, the reloca- tion would have its problems. It's always worst for the first new family that moves in to a fancy-schmancy neighbour- hood. But they understood the importance of fitting in. They'd told themselves, they'd said to each other: well, if we just keep our heads down, try to get along, then you know, maybe folks will meet us half-way. You can't ex- pect them to change their ways overnight just to suit us. We need to work at it, be ambassadors. Be a credit to the species, hold our heads up high. So that's just what they did— they put everything they had into it, but it still wasn't enough. That was the hard part.

From the very first— when the slick realtor had showed them round the house in that faux-friendly, glad-handing way— they'd had misgivings. Mama Bear hated how he looked at her, the way he hardly even bothered to disguise his frequent glances at her heavy low-slung pelvis— as if he could see right through the summery, ill-fitting dress she'd worn specially for the occasion. She felt shamed and exposed; felt all the indignity of the collar and muzzle, the tug of his hand on the chain.

"Get a load of those features," he'd said, leaning in the kitchen doorway, tilting his hat back on his head the better to watch her as she tried to make sense of convection oven, EZ Kleen range hood, griddle, rotisserie. "Just makes you hungry as a hunter, doesn't it?" He was chewing a stick of gum he hadn't bothered to remove since they'd arrived. She could see it now as he worked it between his teeth. It reminded her of a plump grey maggot, the kind you'd find beneath a chunk of dead wood.

Later, in the front room, her heart had felt as heavy as the sleep of hibernation, watching Papa Bear as he nodded his great dense head gravely and earnestly, narrowing his tiny eyes in a show of acumen while Mr. Traynor skimmed over the various clauses of the contract, flicking through the papers haphazardly, not even pretending to explain. When the realtor extended his pen he grappled it determinedly between his callused pads and made his mark. She never forgot the way he looked when glancing up from the contract, proud of the step he'd just taken and yet filled with unassuageable doubts. "That's fine, that's fine," said Jack Traynor, cramming everything into his inside jacket pocket and backing out the door. "You folks are making the right decision, that's for sure." He couldn't wait to get out of there and bank their check.

The first night after the move she could hardly sleep. Midnight came and went, and one a.m., and she was still at the window, gazing over the way at the fine landscaped gardens of their neighbours. Goodness, but those monkey-puzzle trees in the Lockes' arboretum would be so hard to climb... she stopped herself. For shame. She'd already disgraced herself in front of the Lockes, earlier in the day.

Baby had been sent off to play while the grown-ups emptied the furniture van. He'd gone exploring, and a few hours later, after much hollering and head-scratching, she'd found him over in the garden of their nearest neighbours— the Lockes, a charming couple, simply exquisite. They had trees all round the side of the house, Scotch pines, trained willows and those amazing monkey-puzzles, and Baby was in his element, as was all too clear. When she finally tracked him down under the pines he'd just finished Number Two, and was diligently scratching soil over his adorably undersized leaving. "You mind that now," she'd exclaimed, snatching him up— and pausing, entirely out of habit, to check Baby's scat. Good, firm texture; he'd always been a healthy tot, and they hoped he'd thrive in such a good area. Without giving it a second thought, Mama leaned down and sniffed deeply, assessing in an instant the state of her son's digestion: some nibs of corn there still, and a sticky, slightly tarry residue—

"Can we help you?" Several degrees north of glacial.

Hurriedly, with a little snort of surprise, Mama straightened up.

There they were: tall handsome Kenny Locke who was something in advertising, and his wife Mimi, picture-perfect in what looked like real honest-to-goodness Balenciaga. She was so exquisitely turned out, Mama Bear just couldn't believe it; one hand poised hip-high like a model from the glossy magazines, the other hovering at her mouth, where she worried between perfect pearly teeth the tip of her kidskin glove.

Mama introduced herself, held out a paw before catching herself and restricting the movement to a hey-neighbour wave. "And this is Baby," she explained shyly, hoisting him up from off her hip.

"Yes well, it seems Baby's already made himself known," said Mimi Locke, with the merest glance at the discreet plug of infant dung there on the close-mown grass beneath her tree. "If in future you could..." She left the sentence unfinished: it was difficult to say whether this was out of distaste for the subject of the conversation, or for its object.

Mama Bear couldn't apologise fast enough or long enough. In the midst of her explanations she scooped up the offending scrap of ordure, then became hyper-aware of it and held it behind her back, then when she turned to lope back across the lawn she didn't know what to do with it... it was all too shaming for words. Most shaming of all, behind her back she heard them, Mimi and Kenny Locke, their murmurs as she retreated:

"Well, I guess it's true what they say about bears, Meem;" and his rich confident voice sank to a whisper in his wife's petite ear, rising only at the end of the gag: "...but they'll sure shit in the woods." Mimi's tinkling laughter stung like the shards of a flawed crystal glass that shatters in the hand. Later that first evening, upstairs in the bedroom of their new house, Mama Bear cried herself to sleep with that laughter still sounding in her ears.

In the morning there was garbage thrown all over their new lawn, and someone had written in straggly weed killer letters across the grass GO HOME BRUINS.

~

After that, how could they ever really feel at home? Each day was sure to bring some fresh humiliation, a new chance to look down at the tightrope and see the void beneath. For Mama, maybe the final straw had been that disastrous afternoon tea at the Minafers. As the ladies of Scotsford chattered and smiled, Mama Bear had perched on the sofa as if on a hotplate, answering questions in strangled monosyllables while contriving to break a modest yet on the whole representative cross-section of her hostess's best china. "I believe your husband is in show-business, Mrs., ah...?" someone had said— the well-meaning yet essentially dimwitted Missy Scrivener— as she bent, blushing to her burning muzzle, to pick up the pieces.

"Why yes, he's with the circus," she'd replied, struggling to her feet. It was nothing to be ashamed of. Papa was one of the best-paid performers in his field: he drew down thirty grand a year with Krafft's, and they'd hibernated in Florida each year now since '53. How many of these high-toned muckamucks could afford to keep a beach house in the Keys? And yet somewhere behind her back she heard laughter, unsuccessfully smothered.

She swung round, eyeing the rest of the room suspiciously. She saw nothing she could recognise in the whey-pale powdered faces; no hint of fellow-feeling, no shred of empathy. Weren't these people supposed to understand money? Then why couldn't they see it was neutral, after all? Bob Minchin sold limousines to people at his Lincoln dealership downtown. Papa Bear rolled atop his log for them in the big top. Who was to say which one of them ought to have bragging rights over the other?

"Oh, now, let me take those," urged the hostess Mindy Minafer, trying to retrieve the broken cups and plates from her clumsy guest. The sudden movement drew an involuntary grunt from Mama Bear— you couldn't even call it a growl, not really. And the way her claws caught Mindy: that was purely accident. Mindy ought to have known better than to have her hands in there. The hush that fell across the airy, sun-struck drawing-room was none the less petrified for that.

Soon afterwards, people began making their excuses, drifting away in ones and twos until there was only Mama Bear, bidding a bandaged and thin-lipped Mindy goodbye in the miserable expectation this would turn out to be her first, last and only invite to a Scotsford soiree. Which turned out to be true.

After that, Mama mostly stayed home, wishing she could be a wife like any other, wishing she had that role at least to fulfil. She dreamed of how it would feel to be one of those cool, classy WASPish brides you saw on TV: to wait each evening with a freshly mixed Martini against her hi-powered hubby's return. But of course Papa didn't have a regular nine-to-five: work claimed him Easter through till Halloween, the everlasting circuit, life on the road. Nothing for it but to hold her head high, and try to carry on the best she could.

Trips out to the shops— though soon enough she grew sick of negotiating the narrow aisles of the supermarket, overturning pyramids of canned goods and toilet tissue at each incautious turn. Walks with her son out to the park, watching from the shade of the plane trees as the rest of the youngsters played shirts-versus-skins baseball. Trying to explain to Baby as he pleaded with her, puzzled, asking why he couldn't take a turn at bat. In the end whole afternoons and evenings with the blinds drawn, just watching TV, Western shows and daytime soaps and old romantic movies; the hearings of the Senate committee on Ursine Integration, half-a-dozen wrinkled-up old white men barely managing to stay awake while so-called experts pontificated on the kind of problems she faced every day and they would never know, not ever.

When one bright day in June Papa turned up out of the blue, Mama Bear was in her dressing-gown still, though it was half three in the afternoon. She hurried out to the sidewalk as his taxi pulled away, but his first words weren't for her.

"I lay out good money for that gardener, goddamit," he rumbled, scowling at the scutch grass and wild scallions growing through the unwatered lawn, patchwork turf still evident where the burned-in slur had been removed. Mama tried to explain— the neighbours encouraged their dogs to make dirty on the grass when she wasn't watching, and anyway the gardener they'd hired hardly ever showed these days— but he waved it away with an angry paw. "Working my ass off so this place can look like some damn pauper shack when I get home..." He lurched off inside the house, Mama Bear hurrying after. Across the way, curtains twitched.

All that evening he was mute, unapproachable. Finally Mama Bear came right out and asked the question.

"No... no, Mama, everything is not all right," he said heavily. He squinted through his glass of bourbon, the lamplight reflecting yellow in his baleful eye. "Everything is going pretty much to shit, if you really want to know."

Mama Bear flinched, as always, at the word. "Honey!"

"Honey's all dried up," he said, tipping back the whole tumbler full of bourbon in a single blink-inducing draught. "Nothing left but the ol' ca-ca now. The ol' poopy-doop."

"Don't talk that way," she told him, scared a little, not wanting to hear what else he might say. "Oh, you don't know how much I've been looking forward to having you home, Papa, even if it is only for a week—"

"It isn't a week's leave," he said, heavily. He rose to his feet, staggered a little, made for the corner bar to replenish his glass. Without turning to face her, he said: "It's mandatory leave. *Indefinite* mandatory leave."

"I don't understand...?" Mama tried to face him, look into his eyes, to find out what it might mean, all of it. Papa pushed past her, not roughly but not tenderly either, shambled back to the sofa, collapsed as if he'd taken a tranquiliser dart to the flank.

"I blew it, Mama." Staring at the ceiling, where cobwebs hung from the chandelier. "Matinee performance in Schenectady. I was waiting to go on... I just turned round and walked right out the big top. Couldn't go on. Just... couldn't."

"Honey? What?"

Papa Bear held a paw up as if to forestall her; let it fall. "I just *couldn't.*"

She felt she should understand without having to ask, felt ashamed because she didn't. "Was it... did someone say something? Did you get into a fight again?"

"I just..." For the longest time he tried to say it. Not even another slug of bourbon could loosen his tongue. "Ah, what the hell. You don't understand."

Now the tears came, she couldn't help it. "I want you to help me understand!" Wanted him to hold her, to say, it's all right, it's gonna be okay. Instead he sat back, stared at the ceiling, said as if to no-one:

"You'll never know what it cost me, to do that every day. To go through with that whole... that whole charade."

"They pay you good!" She was sobbing openly now. "The best!"

"They make me jump through hoops," he said, more in resignation than in bitterness. "They make me jump through their goddamn hoops, each and every day, and there's not one goddamn thing I can do about it, because they own me. Bought and paid for."

"They don't own you! They pay you a wage! A *good* wage!"

"They own my ass, Mama." Correcting her heavily. "They want me to do handstands— I do handstands. End of story. And one day— one day..." He was searching for a form of words to make it more comprehensible to her, or perhaps to himself. "This one afternoon in Schenectady, I was checking out the apparatus— the log, the hoops, the podiums, all set up in the middle of the ring— and I just said the hell with it. You know?" He drained his tumbler, set it down with a crack on the glass tabletop. "The hell with it. Walked. Lay on the bunk in my goddamn caravan, stayed there till the boss came knocking." For the first time he met her eyes, blinking owlishly as one who emerges into bright sunlight from the back of a deep dark cave. "And here I am. Indefinite mandatory leave." He snorted mirthlessly, got up to pour himself another bourbon.

Mama Bear tried to make sense of it all. "You've been overdoing things— working too hard..."

"I've been doing what I do," said her husband bleakly into the middle distance, one paw on the bottle, the other bracing himself against the cocktail bar. "I've been dancing to their tune. All my life, Mama. Now the music's stopped, and there isn't a chair left for me to sit in."

~

And so their dream move to Scotsford turned all the way nightmare, and there was nothing anyone could do about it. For the remainder of that evening Mama Bear alternately cried and pleaded, while Papa drank steadily and without appreciable effect, until all of a sudden he let out an enormous roar and sent the glass-top table flying against the farther wall. After that she ran crying up to bed, tiptoed down hours after in the predawn grey to find her husband collapsed on the couch, breathing stertorously through his wide open mouth. Looking down at him, she didn't know what to think— what to feel, even. She didn't know whether she wanted things to be the way they'd been before, or what she wanted. Just not this.

The weather turned hot and humid in the weeks that followed, those enervating dog days of summer when the only sounds across suburbia's lazy lawns are the hissing of sprinklers and the elastic crack of tennis ball on catgut. When French windows are wedged permanently open, and ice clinks welcomingly in pitchers of cool iced tea and daiquiris fetched out to poolside. Inside the dream homes, sweltering Negro staff polished and cleaned and laundered, while life moved out on to the decks and patios. Recumbent in its thousand sweet suntraps, Scotsford stretched out in the heat, grew blasé and lethargic, tilted its face to the sweltering rays and adjusted its sunglasses.

In the house of the bears, things were different. No French window was left ajar against the heat, and all the blinds were drawn in the daytime. No one came in or out of the house: the cleaner, Hortense, had long since been let go, along with the gardener, Booker T. The only person who seemed to be let in still was the delivery boy from Biddle's Market. Pressed on the details by Missy Scrivener, the Biddle's boy would only say that things were kinda gloomy inside, and they mostly left his money laid out ready on the kitchen table.

Yes, and through the crack in the kitchen door Mama Bear would watch the kid come in, glance nervously around, leave the boxes on the table, grab his cash and scoot. She told herself she watched to make sure he left the groceries and was off on his way with no shenanigans, didn't steal or poke his nose in where it wasn't wanted... but a part of her she couldn't really get to, let alone acknowledge, probably watched him because he was the only thing worth watching in all that gloomy house. The only creature moving at the noon.

More and more Papa was sleeping through the hot hours, midday till six. When he rose, he'd mostly just lie on his bed, staring at the ceiling; only when the sun was slipping down behind the roof of the Lockes' house would he even consider stirring. One evening Mama Bear heard a fearsome crash from out back: running to the French windows she saw Papa sprawled amidst the wreck of the swing set on the lawn. The tube-aluminum frame of the garden furniture was all wrenched out of shape, bowed and bent beneath his helpless bulk. Papa, she thought, though it was dusk already and getting hard to see, was crying. That evening in bed, desperate to restore what she could of his dignity and self-esteem, she presented herself to him. After a brief humiliating interlude of strain and poke he rolled away, as if from the failure of some trick he'd learned once for a special performance, but long since forgotten how to do properly.

After that, they mostly kept out of each other's way. Papa hit the bottle with increasing frequency, and Mama began to find herself doing odd little things around the house, things she couldn't always have consciously explained but which just felt right. She sent Baby out to the woods to gather dry leaves and twigs, which she strewed throughout the rooms. She found herself one day dragging her claws through the jazzy patterned wallpaper, leaving a cross-hatched pattern of parallel score-marks clean down to the plaster underneath. Once, she came to as if from a stupor to find herself squatting to stool in the darkest corner of the dining room.

With no air blowing through, the house began to smell old and musty, like the back of a deep hibernation cave. Papa's empties were mounting up around the study, and it reeked of stale booze in there— if failure were to have a scent, it would surely be the sour stink that lingers round a sticky flyblown liquor bottle. Mama's occasional indiscretions, mimicked eagerly by Baby now, lent an earthy tainted smell to the dining room, and drew flies in the hundreds in their own right. Those doors were kept shut; other rooms they wandered through in a kind of desultory fretfulness, as if looking for something but unable to remember quite what it was. Curling up for a while, fast asleep in the fever heat, forgetting in the instant of their waking what they'd just that second dreamed. Passing each other without a word, without a touch.

For the most part the bears ate alone now, each one wandering through to the kitchen and raiding the refrigerator or the pantry shelves. One day— one afternoon of pregnant rumbling thunder in the far-off hills— Mama went to the Westinghouse and found it empty. Only condiments and rancid month-old butter, was all. She stared into the chilly glowing void for what must have been a long while, till the buzz of the refrigerator motor kicking in woke her with a little start from her stupor.

Dully she hunted through the cupboards, found nothing that spoke to her rumbling slavering hunger. There was a packet of porridge oats, which she tried dry and spat out. Tipping the contents into a saucepan, she added water and watched while the mess bubbled up on the greasy, crusted stove. The smell drew the rest of the family, and in their various stages of wakefulness they all sat around the table and waited for the porridge to boil.

Finally it was ready. Mama dolloped the grey goop into large Tupperware mixing bowls and placed them on the table. Baby took the bowl in both hands and lapped eagerly at its contents, only to recoil in shock and pain. "Too hot!" he squeaked. The dropped bowl skittered around on the tabletop, coming to rest in a glutinous blob of spilled porridge. Mama winced internally— she'd meant to check the temperature. She'd meant to order food; she'd meant to do a lot of things, one way and another. She was so forgetful nowadays...

Impervious to scalds, Papa tasted his portion and spat it on to the floor. "Needs sweetening," he grumbled. "Don't we have any damn sugar in this house?"

Mama was fairly sure they hadn't— in fact, she vividly recalled pouring the best part of a packet down her maw, crusting her muzzle with sweet granules as she tore apart what was left of the bag with her rough tongue— but she went through the motions of looking anyway. "Okay, that's it," ordered Papa. "In the car, now."

And so the whole family piled into the station wagon, which Papa proceeded to drive all herky-jerky down to the store. Cars threw on the brakes and honked horns as Papa shot one intersection after another, jumped a red light downtown, made a huge and illegal U-turn across the flower-bedded midway on Main to park up outside Biddle's.

Inside, Mama hurried timorously down the aisles in Papa's snarling wake, wincing as he swept the entire contents of the honey shelf into his trolley with a swipe of his paw. At the checkout there was another contretemps, when the girl at the register wanted to see some ID for the roughly scrawled check he'd presented. "You see the check?" he growled. "You see the *name* on the check?"

"Um, that's, er, Bear, yes I do, sir," confirmed the nervous teenager.

Papa Bear loosened his collar, pushed back his trilby, and thrust his face to within an inch of the checkout girl's. She recoiled, tipping over her castor-wheeled stool. "Well, here's my ID, then," he said, and barged his trolley on through and out to the car. Scalded by shame, Mama backed away, trying to keep up with her husband while apologising to the gathering knot of Biddle's staff.

And so, after another death-defying chariot ride through the downtown, they came once more to a squealing halt in their own driveway, demolishing a flowerbed and knocking over their own mailbox in the process. Laden down with honeypots, they staggered the few yards from car to front door, left ajar in the haste of their departure. In the houses and gardens of their neighbours, this excursion had not gone unnoticed. As the front door banged shut after the bears, a murmur of adverse comment blew up and down the avenue like a dry harsh Santa Ana.

Inside, Papa was heading for the kitchen when he came to a sudden halt. Head up, he sniffed the stale hot air. "Honey?" asked Mama Bear, bumping in to him from behind.

"Nah..." He shrugged, and carried on into the kitchen. Where they both stopped and gaped.

The porridge had been flung all over the walls and ceilings. Great globs of it dripped down to the spattered floor; over by the back door, Baby's little dish, still stuck with its gloopy contents, slid slowly down the wall like a Tupperware snail.

Mama let out a single barking sob. Papa, meanwhile, pushed past her into the dining room, rumbling "What the...?"

In the dining room there was nothing; nothing, except the certain knowledge that some uninvited guest had passed that way not minutes before. Call it a spoor: every animal leaves some kind of track, after all. Following his nose, Papa hurried through to the living room.

Pushing aside the room dividers, he yelped in harsh surprise. All of the cushions on all of the chairs lay ripped apart, like so many chickens torn by the fox. Feathers fell through the air still, settling on the leaf-strewn carpet, the denuded chairs; settling on the triangular-bladed kitchen knife that had doubtless done the damage. The knife from their very own kitchen, part of a set. When everything had been perfect, back in the beginning.

The trail was so fresh, though, it drew Papa on with hardly time for a glance at the damage. Onwards, up the stairs to Baby's room. At the turn of the landing, he stopped and waited for Mama to catch up. With a jerk of his huge heavy head he indicated the door to their son's room. Together they moved towards it.

And there she was: the culprit, the interloper, the crafty assassin of hearth and home. Picture perfect, Shirley Temple in ribbons and curls, the Locke girl, little Goldie

Locke, caught mid-bounce on Baby's mussed-up bed.

It was Mama who moved first of all, though she hardly knew she was doing it: a lunge forward and the beginnings of a roar, and then she got wedged in between Papa and the doorframe, luckily for little Goldie, maybe. But even a doorway full of angry bear didn't seem to shake the Locke girl's composure. She completed the bounce by landing on her little keister, shook her hair from her eyes and regarded the bears with the haughty self-possession of a born aristocrat.

"What... what..." Mama couldn't even get the words out; Papa was still mute in the grip of some complicated emotion. It was left to Baby, pushing in between their legs, to ask the obvious, indeed the necessary question: "What are you doing on my bed?"

"You left the front door wiiide open." A lisping singsong, befitting her gingham and curls. "Stupid bears."

All three of the bears were shocked into silence. It was as if, after all the whispering campaigns and sly talk exchanged behind their backs, Scotsford was finally showing its hand.

"Stupid bruins," Goldie Locke continued happily. "Stupid, stupid bruins. You smell."

Mama opened her mouth, and shut it again.

"You do so!" The little girl answered the thought, rather than the unspoken words. "You do ca-ca in the dining room! Where you eat your dinner!"

Mama looked round at her husband. He was staring, not at the girl but at her. Hastily he looked away, as did she.

"Stinky, stinky bruins..." An extemporised schoolyard rhyme, complete with mocking rise and fall. "And you got leaves and branches everywhere round the house! And old bottles! And ca-ca! You're like... tramps!"

The three bears shrank together.

"My mummy said all bruins smell, so I came inside to see. And you do smell." The vindication made her giggle, and she lifted a hand to her mouth. Politely, as she'd been taught by her mother. "You're stinky. Stinky poo-poo." And then it was simply too funny for words, and she laughed at them, right to their faces.

Recovering from her laughing jag, hiccupping a little, the little girl regarded the bears. "I wanna go home now," she said. "It smells in here." She got up from the bed. The bears made no move.

Goldie Locke frowned. "You get out of the way," she told them. "Stinky bears. Go on now! Or I'll tell my daddy."

Still the bears did not move. They stood as one and looked at her.

"My daddy says you should all be in a *zoo!*"

The Zee word.

At his mother's side, little Baby burst into tears. Slowly, without taking her eyes off the girlchild, Mama lowered a paw to the top of his head.

"He says you get money by tricks, and you stink, and you belong in a zoo. I don't wanna stay here, it's stinky and I feel sick to my tummy." She glared at them in unconcealed disgust. "You let me go past, you hear?"

What did they feel, Mama, Papa, Baby? What stirred in the thick gamy meat of their hearts as the little blonde girl mocked and insulted them? What might their reaction have been, had they only found it in their nature to react?

Impatiently, Goldie Locke stamped one perfect sandaled foot on the unvacuumed carpet, lifting a little puff of dust. "Get *back!*" she ordered, with a shrillness that brooked no contradiction. Every ringmaster's whip that ever cracked, in that command; every lick from the licking stick.

As if by magic, the three bears shuffled back a pace. With all the confidence in the world, little Goldie Locke stepped towards them.

~

Later that evening, on the piney hillside above Scotsford,

Papa Bear paused for breath near the top of the ridge. He'd been carrying Baby on his shoulders, and now he set him down on the sandy ground while he waited for Mama to catch them up.

Hampered by the... well, by the hamper she was carrying, plus the sundry bags and coats and what-nots, Mama lumbered after them up the hill. Her dress was torn from pushing through the bushes back down in the valley, but it had been necessary— very much necessary— that their departure go unobserved. Hence the unconventional route through the back garden.

Puffing a little, she finally caught up with the boys in the little clearing near the hilltop. Gratefully she let go her various burdens, just in time for Baby to come barrelling straight into them as he forward-rolled over to greet her. Everything was sent flying, and a good half of the stuff went rolling off down the hill. She made only the most perfunctory attempts to retrieve it. Instead, she gathered up her son and turned to her husband, watching for his response.

Papa was staring back down the hill at the town they'd left behind. Scotsford lay bathed in the super-radiant glow of a nuclear sunset: across the hushed and lovely suburb pools winked blue, patio barbecues wafted savoury smells into the evening air, porch lights glittered against the gathering dusk. From up on the hill you could no longer hear the vague hum of conversations, the hi-fis playing Mantovani; you couldn't feel the taut thin lines of tension that lay behind it all, like guy ropes braced to hold the big top high.

The big bear looked down at the houses of the humans for the longest time, till the sun was finally down behind the farther hillside. Ruminatively he ran a claw under his collar and tie, ripped them away almost without thinking. Ditched the trilby. And then, with a perfect spontaneity that made Mama Bear forget for a moment all the trials and tribulations down the weeks and months and years— forget the horrors they'd left back in the Scotsford house, even— he pitched seven perfect roll-overs, and stood triumphant at the end, stood tall and proud and bearlike once again. Mama barked her approval, and Baby mimicked his papa; they romped and sported in the clearing, all of them, tearing up the rich loam and pine needles underfoot, cloaking themselves with the stink of nature once more. And then, as the night birds cried and the huge yellow moon rose up ahead of them, they lumbered off one by one into the forest and were gone.

Author's Note: Steve Duffy

You can Google, if you want to, the source of the obsession that lies behind this story. imdb.com/title/tt0862707/ will take you to the IMDb entry for the Coronet live-action featurette "Goldilocks and the Three Bears" (1958), an Eisenhower-era twee-fest featuring a winsome skipping moppet and three real live bears, dressed in human clothes and tugged into position by wires; thin, cruel-looking wires. Anthropomorphism, then: a longstanding fascination, with its origins in our attempts to make the world comprehensible, to bring it alive on our own terms. (Also, as a footnote, I'm guaranteed to laugh at any joke which begins "An [ANIMAL] walks into a bar, and says to the bartender...") This, combined with my love of the David Lynch school of American picket-fence surrealism, must have been working at the back of my mind when I came up with "Bears;" not so much an allegory, because as Tolkien says, "I much prefer history— true or feigned— with its varied applicability to the thought and experience of readers. I think that many confuse applicability with allegory, but the one resides in the freedom of the reader, and the other in the purposed domination of the author."

About the Authors

Lynda E. Rucker is an American writer born and raised in the South and currently living in Dublin, Ireland. Her first short story collection, *The Moon Will Look Strange*, was recently published by Karōshi Books. Her fiction has appeared in such places as *The Magazine of Fantasy & Science Fiction*, *The Mammoth Book of Best New Horror*, *The Year's Best Dark Fantasy and Horror*, *Postscripts*, *Shadows and Tall Trees*, *Nightmare Magazine*, and *Supernatural Tales*. She is a regular columnist for *Black Static*.

Cory J. Herndon is the author of numerous novels, including the *Magic: the Gathering Ravnica Cycle*, and his most recent published work is the short story "Storbeck's Gold" appearing in the Omnium Gatherum horror anthology *Fortune: Lost and Found*. By day he is the Senior Narrative Designer on Carbine Studios' upcoming MMORPG WildStar. Cory lives in southern California with his wife, author S.P. Miskowski, and their senior feline consultant Remo the Cat.

Kate Jonez writes dark fantasy fiction. Her debut novel *Candy House* published by Evil Jester Press is available at Amazon in print and ebook. *Ceremony of Flies* is forthcoming from Dark Fuse April 2014.

Kate is a student of all things scary and when she isn't writing she loves to collect objects for her cabinet of curiosities, research obscure and strange historical figures, and photograph weirdness in Southern California where she lives with a very nice man and a little dog who is also very nice but could behave a little bit better. You can read free short stories at her website at katejonez.com

Johnny Worthen grew up in the high desert snows and warm summer winds of the Wasatch Mountains. He graduated with a B.A. in English, minor in Classics and a Master's in American Studies from the University of Utah. After a series of businesses and adventures, including years abroad and running his own bakery, Worthen found himself drawn to the only thing he ever wanted to do— write. And write he does. When he's not pounding on his keyboard or attending conferences, Worthen spends his time with his wife and two boys in Sandy, Utah.

James Everington mainly writes dark, supernatural fiction, although he occasionally takes a break and writes dark, non-supernatural fiction. His second collection of such tales, *Falling Over*, is out now from Infinity Plus. He has a black cat and cream carpets, which shows how much thought he puts into those parts of his life that aren't book-related.

Oh and he drinks Guinness, if anyone's asking. You can find out what James is currently up to at his Scattershot Writing site: jameseverington.blogspot.co.uk

S.P. Miskowski's debut novel, *Knock Knock* and her first novella, *Delphine Dodd* were finalists for a Shirley Jackson Award. Both books are part of *The Skillute Cycle*, which includes two more novellas: *Astoria*, and *In the Light*. *The Skillute Cycle* is published by Omnium Gatherum Media.

Miskowski has received a Swarthout Prize for fiction and two National Endowment for the Arts Fellowships. Her stories have appeared in *Other Voices*, *Identity*

Theory, Supernatural Tales, Horror Bound Magazine, Fine Madness, and in the Omnium Gatherum anthology *Detritus.* Her non-fiction has appeared in *Nightmare Magazine.* She lives in California with her husband, writer Cory J. Herndon. You can contact her and read excerpts from her books at her blog, Daughters of Catastrophe: d-o-cat.blogspot.com

Brent Michael Kelley lives in Northern Wisconsin with his wife, son, and dogs. When he isn't writing or making wine, he likes sitting around a campfire and telling wild stories that may never have happened. He keeps his readers informed about his perfectly normal — and 100% legal— activities at brentmichaelkelley.com. His next book, Chuggie and the Prisoner Gods, is on the way. Go Pack!

Mary Borsellino is a quiet extrovert and an obnoxious introvert, writes anything she can find an excuse for, and works for a charity in Australia as a day job. Her website is maryborsellino.com and she likes it when strangers email her to say hi.

Ennis Drake's short fiction has appeared in various publications online and in print, including: "Love: The Breath of Eagleray", at Underland Press (publisher of Jeff VanderMeer's "Finch", John Shirley's "In Extremis", Brian Evenson's "Last Days", among others); "The Dark That Keeps Her", published in *Twisted Legends,* an anthology from Pill Hill Press (honorably mentioned in Ellen Datlow's *Best Horror of the Year, Vol. 2*); and "The Fishing of Dahlia", published in the Bram Stoker-nominated and Black Quill Award winning *Horror Library Volume 4.* "The Fishing of Dahlia" also received an honorable mention in Ellen Datlow's *Best Horror of the Year, Vol. 3.*

Most recently, from Word Horde publications, "The Butcher, The Baker, The Candlestick-Maker", appeared in the anthology *Tales of Jack the Ripper*, edited by Ross Lockhart. Upcoming work includes featured stories in *The Book of Cthulhu III*, as well as *Giallo Fantastique* (also from Word Horde).

His novella, *Twenty-Eight Teeth of Rage*, was released May 31st, 2012, from Omnium Gatherum Media, a finalist for the Shirley Jackson Award, and the collected novelettes, "The Day and the Hour" and "Drone", were released by Omnium Gatherum Media in Feb. of 2013.

Mercedes M. Yardley is a dark fantasist who wears stilettos and red lipstick. She is the author of the short story collection *Beautiful Sorrows*, the novella *Apocalyptic Montessa and Nuclear Lulu: A Tale of Atomic Love* and her debut novel *Nameless*. Her website is mercedesyardley.com

Steve Duffy's work has appeared in numerous magazines and anthologies in Europe and North America. His most recent collection of weird short stories, *The Moment Of Panic* was published in 2013, and includes the International Horror Guild award-winning short story, "The Rag-and-Bone Men". Steve lives in North Wales.

www.ingramcontent.com/pod-product-compliance
Lightning Source LLC
Chambersburg PA
CBHW060225180626
46813CB00007B/2962